Sink

Bazza jerked awake. Fear iced his blood. Where the hell was he? His muscles tensed. How come he was in such a situation? The way to stay safe was to sleep rough, in dank out of the way spots. Old buildings, under bridges or subways, anywhere out of the wind. An old clothing bin. If you could get into it, and out again.

But Bazza's luck has changed — a job, a bed, three square meals a day. And Earl ... the first real friend he's had. Things are definitely looking up, though it's still not always safe ...

The muted scrape of steel on rock exploded him into full wakefulness. His eyes snapped open as his feet hit the deck. One leap and he was through the doorway into the wheelhouse. His eyes confirmed what he already knew. The boat was in deadly danger. He bellowed back down the short stairway. 'Hit the deck! Fast!'

Ron Bunney was born in Geraldton, Western Australia. He has worked as a farmer, a salesman and a crayfisherman, and travelled widely throughout Australia. More recently, he has worked on a number of series for children's television, including 'Falcon Island', and his book, *Eye of the Eagle* (Fremantle Arts Centre Press, 1995), was named a Notable Australian Children's Book by the Children's Book Council of Australia.

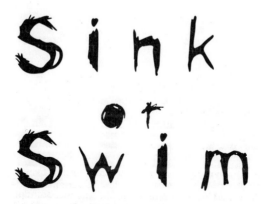

Sink or Swim

ron bunney

FREMANTLE ARTS CENTRE PRESS

First published 1999 by
FREMANTLE ARTS CENTRE PRESS
193 South Terrace (PO Box 320), South Fremantle
Western Australia 6162.
http://www.facp.iinet.net.au

Consultant Editor Alwyn Evans.
Cover Designer Marion Duke.
Production Manager Cate Sutherland.

Typeset by Fremantle Arts Centre Press
and printed by Australian Print Group

National Library of Australia
Cataloguing-in-Publication data:

Bunney, Ron, 1929– .
  Sink or swim.

  ISBN 1 86368 238 4.

  I. Title.

A823.3

The State of Western Australia has made an investment in this project
through ArtsWA in association with the Lotteries Commission.

1

Bazza crept through thick beach scrub and surveyed the shack. He'd seldom needed such caution before. All of the shacks he came across were deserted — until his fright, two hot, hungry days further south.

He'd been asleep in the only bedroom of a shack, when the locked and bolted front door smashed open. Bazza had entered a few hours earlier via the window above his head. He was still congratulating himself for leaving it open. It took him only seconds to slip out and melt into the scrub. From its protective screen, he heard smashing and crashing going on inside.

Apparently, they didn't find what they were looking for. When the two men emerged, they were almost empty handed. The expressions on their faces made Bazza even more relieved that he'd eluded them. The younger man carried a plastic bag. It contained the few tins of food Bazza had ferreted out and left on the table. The middle aged man had a rifle. Both were tough, hard men. Bazza knew the type. He didn't stick around.

With that memory fresh in his mind, he took no chances. He circled around through the scrub and looked down onto the beach. Scrapings and thumpings were the only sounds he could hear. He spotted their source. A young guy, stripped to the waist, carried a craypot from the heap on his ute and added it to a stack at the water's edge.

Bazza's stomach growled. It reminded him of what he had to do. Now! And quick! Risky, but he was desperate.

He slid back through the bush and approached the shack's open door. The guy lived here. He would have food on hand. A quick glance told him there were no other occupants. He slipped in and searched the cupboards.

Earl Griffson stacked the fiftieth pot by the water's edge. He straightened and massaged a sore spot on his shoulder. Another forty to go. Then, he had to get them out to his moored boat. He took a deep breath. At least he'd passed the halfway mark on this stage of the job. Getting the gear into the water was always a hard slog. He felt hard done by, but the feeling was short lived. He was his own man. Made his own decisions. He'd been told what to do for far too long. As the youngest child of four he knew what it was to be the knucklehead on the end of the line.

Right now, Earl's main problem was he still had no deckhand and it was November the ninth. Bait-up day was the fourteenth. First pull of the season was the fifteenth.

Cliffhead anchorage had no jetty. It was a curve of white sand and a patch of reef-protected sea, thirty kilometres from the nearest town. No wonder he had trouble keeping a decky, at least one with an ounce of commonsense. Even the no-hopers only took it on as a last resort. It was too far from the boozer and the birds.

Earl shrugged. He'd find someone. There must be others like himself who didn't fit the mould. He'd make another trip to the factory in Dongara and see who had turned up. Time had run out, he could no longer be choosy. He would take whoever he could get.

He grimaced, turned and plodded through the sand towards his shack. The sun had a sting in it and the southerly was slow in arriving. He cursed the wind when he was pulling pots. Today he would welcome its coolness. He needed a long cold drink and something to eat. After a spell he'd get stuck into it again.

His shack crouched in a hollow between a small scrub-covered sandhill and the shoulder of limestone that gave the locality its name. No garden softened its outline. No frilly curtains shielded its windows. Earl had built it and it looked like him, practical and not scared of hard work.

His bare feet made little noise as he walked through the front door. Shock halted him. 'Find what you're lookin' for?'

A kid jerked away from the fridge, crouched defensively and faced the doorway. His escape route blocked, the kid used the only missile he had. He hurled a carton of milk at Earl's head, then lunged in its wake. Earl swayed aside. The carton sailed through the doorway. The kid charged for the gap. Earl shot back and crashed his shoulder into the boy's chest. The kid grunted and sprawled amongst the legs of the table and chairs. Bread and cheese spilled from his arms. He scrambled to his feet and groped for a weapon. His hand gripped a chair back.

Earl closed and grabbed a fistful of shirt. The kid slammed his knee at Earl's groin. Earl twisted and took the blow on his thigh. He then hurled the boy against the wall. Air jarred from his lungs and he slid to the floor.

Earl stood over him but kept a gap between them. The boy drew back his legs for a double footed kick. Earl wasn't falling for that. He'd been there, done that.

The kid cringed. His body sagged. He looked like a whipped dog. Earl relaxed a little and wished he hadn't been so hard on him. He took a deep breath and stepped back a pace. 'Okay. What's it all about?'

The kid took a moment or two to regain his breath. 'I … was … hungry.'

'What's the matter with your tongue?'

The kid looked puzzled. 'Nothin'. Why?'

'You could've asked. I would've given you a feed.'

'So you say.' A surly, belligerent look settled on the kid's face.

Earl studied him for a moment, then stooped and picked up the bread and cheese. He put it on the table, then crossed to the fridge. He took out some sliced meat and two cans of coke. He shut the fridge door.

He put one can on the table in front of a chair. Then he sat at the opposite side of the table. He popped his can, lifted it to his lips and drank. It was a long drink and he sat back in his chair as he finished. 'Ahhh! Needed that.'

The boy watched every action. Earl's attention, though less direct, also missed nothing. He noticed a change in the boy's body language. It now reminded him of a dog, beaten but not totally cowed. Hackles were still aroused. He gestured towards the food on the table. 'Come on, get some into ya.'

The kid glanced towards the food. Hunger rumbled his stomach. He started to rise, then hesitated. Earl didn't move. He rose and slid onto the chair at the opposite end of the table. His gaze fastened on Earl, he groped for the food. Found some bread and crammed it into his mouth. He swallowed without chewing. It hurt his throat.

'Slow down. It's not gunna run away.'

The boy again bit into the thick slice of bread. This time he chewed it.

'Where'd you come from?'

'What's it to you?' The answer came through the bread in his mouth.

'Not much. No skin off my nose where you come from.' Earl slid a solid paring knife across the table. 'For the cheese.'

The kid grabbed it with his fist around the handle. The pointed blade protruded aggressively forward. Despite the sudden tension, Earl maintained an outward calm. He continued to fold a slice of bread around a piece of cheese.

After a moment's indecision, the boy changed his grip and hacked off a chunk of cheese. He bit into it and followed it with a bite of meat.

'What's your name?' Earl's voice was even, not sharp or aggressive.

'What you wanna know for?'

'Better than sayin' hey you.'

The boy chewed on for a while, then swallowed. 'Barry. Bazza.'

Earl nodded. 'Mine's Earl. Who calls you Bazza? Your old man?'

'Got no old man.'

'Who you runnin' from?'

'Not him that's for sure. I split. Long time ago.'

Earl figured that 'a long time' depended on how old the person was. How old was this kid? Fifteen? Sixteen? 'Who's him?'

'Mum's boyfriend. Bastard! Should've done him in.' With an aggressive movement Bazza snatched up the knife and plunged it into the block of cheese. Hotness prickled his eyes. He forced it back. No way! Crying was dead! The last time was when that crazy bastard bashed him senseless.

That wasn't the first time he'd ended up in hospital with 'unexplained' injuries. But it was the first time he'd had guts enough to do something about it. He cleared out as soon as he was mobile. He wasn't narked at the hospital staff. They were kind to him. But if he stayed, his mother would come crying and drag him home 'after his accident'. In hindsight, he realised that when previous injuries and broken bones had put him in hospital, he'd been too young and scared to protest or realise it wasn't normal. His early memories were all about 'accidents'.

His mother had probably gone through more boyfriends since that bastard. He neither knew nor cared. No one else had broken him, even during the hardest times on the street. There was no way memories would break him now.

An uneasy silence dragged as they both stared at the knife. Earl spoke first, he could see the kid was doing it tough. 'He worth goin' to jail for?'

Bazza thought a moment, then shook his head. He plucked the knife from the cheese and lay it on the table. He took alternate bites of bread and cheese and ate steadily. Finally drank from the can of coke. Tension seeped from him.

Earl finished his drink. 'Where're you headed?'

'Dunno.'

'Where've you come from?'

Bazza shrugged. 'South.' He drained his can then bit into more bread and cheese.

Earl helped himself to more food. He ate easily. He was in no hurry.

Bazza finally stopped eating and looked up. 'You gunna dob me in?'

'Nope.'

Bazza was silent, then flicked a glance towards the door. 'Better go then.'

'If that's what you want.' Earl appraised the boy's condition, saw the dark around his eyes, his gaunt look, the crumpled, stained state of his clothes. He inclined his head in the direction of the shack's second room. 'Bed in there if you wanna crash.'

Bazza looked from Earl to the doorway and back again. Expressions of belief and disbelief played across his face. He covered them by getting to his feet. He walked wide of Earl, glanced inside, then back. Earl hadn't moved.

'You for real?' Bazza couldn't figure him. Seemed like he was up front but Bazza trusted no one. No one gave you anything for nothing. What was he up to? Was he trying to corner him in the room?

'Do I look like a ghost?'

Bazza's thoughts flicked to their recent tussle. Felt pain from new bruises. Earl *was* for real. Right now, he looked relaxed and non threatening. Bazza glanced back into the room. His hesitation disappeared at the sight of the bed. Numb with fatigue, he stumbled towards it. Maybe ten or twenty minutes?

Earl remained seated. He heard the bed creak. Thoughts floated through his mind. Would it work? Was it worth the gamble? The idea was obviously flawed. Kid looked as though he'd gone feral. And yet ... Gambles sometimes worked. Gut feeling played a large part in it.

Sometime later Earl got to his feet and walked to the bedroom door. The boy was sprawled on top of the bed. He appeared to be asleep but there was a tenseness about him. He looked as relaxed as a coiled spring.

Bazza snapped to full alert. From habit, he slept light. It usually gave him enough rest to maintain his waking hours. A voice had shattered that rest. He jerked his knees to his chest. Both feet primed to lash out with a double kick. The shock tactic had got him out of tight spots in the past.

He slept in the dregs when he roamed the city streets. Learned the hard way it didn't pay to sleep in the same place for too many nights in a row. Sometimes he crawled into a large cardboard box and shivered himself to sleep. If you could call it sleep. Unfortunately, there was always some creep poking around, looking for a boy to take home for the night. Then kick him out when he finished with him. Mid-winter, the prospect of a warm bed for at least one night, and a few bucks in his pocket, almost broke him. Some kids gave in. Reckoned it was the lesser of many evils.

The voice came again. Bazza recognised it as Earl's. 'Easy, Bazza … no one's gunna hurt you.'

Bazza uncurled. Sat up. Sleep-gummed eyes adjusted to the gloom. He spotted Earl standing a pace back from the bed. He was surprised by the room's darkness. Had he slept that long?

'Hungry?'

Bazza's stomach answered him before he nodded.

'Made a pot of stew. Interested?'

His nose accepted messages and Bazza nodded again.

'It's on the table.' Earl turned and walked from the room.

He was seated at the far end of the table when Bazza snailed into the kitchen. He flicked a glance towards the outside doorway. Checking escape routes was routine. The door was closed. A light southerly breeze introduced a degree of coolness. It would be a cold night in the bush.

Earl indicated the heaped plate across the table. Whisps of steam hazed from its surface. Gravy, meat and onion smells filled the air. Chunks of potato and other vegetables jutted from the pile.

He should do a runner, but Jeez! That food! Mesmerised, he slid onto the chair in front of the plate. He shot a nervous glance at Earl. Earl was chewing on a mouthful and again dug his fork into the stew. Bazza dug in his own fork.

A forty watt fluorescent light flickered from the ceiling and an engine purred somewhere outside. Bazza emptied his plate in record time and cleaned it with a crust of bread.

Earl had nearly finished. He studied the kid as he asked, 'Wanna job?'

Bazza paused with the piece of crust headed for his mouth. He stifled his surprise and replaced the expression on his face with the habitual surly one. 'Doin' what?'

'Deckying.'

'Dunno nothin' about it.'

'Neither did I when I started.'

Bazza hesitated. It was a question he'd never been asked before. And that wasn't the only reason. This guy puzzled him. Perhaps he did mean what he was saying. Then again, he could be more devious than the people he'd come across. Watch it, Bazz. Watch it.

'You dunno anythin' about me.'

'Might not have read a million books but I like to think I can read people.'

'What's that supposed to mean?'

'I need someone who can keep their wits about them. Had a guy on happy weed once. Have had several in fact. Long-time users, couldn't remember anythin' for more than five minutes. Sea doesn't let you make mistakes. Not often anyway.'

'So?'

'I reckon you've still got your head together.'

Bazza thought about that for a while. Felt a strange tingle. He dismissed it, then said, 'I might've done … things.'

'It's what you do from now on that counts.'

Bazza's interest rekindled. Hope resurfaced. Was it worth a try? Hard on its heels came caution and suspicion rolled into one. The feeling hurt, as though he wanted to hope, but was afraid to. He forced casualness into his voice. 'Think I can handle it?'

'You'll learn. Be hard at first. Damned hard, but your muscles will get used to it.'

A legitimate job! It was almost beyond belief. Bazza forced the question out. He had a vague idea it was a question you asked. It might sort things out. If the guy was having him on, talk of money would make him back off. 'What'll you pay me?'

'Standard contract rate for deckes. I'll call the factory and check on that. The more we catch, the more you earn. The more we both earn.'

Bazza sat with eyes downcast. The concept of paid work was hard to accept. It was something he believed could never happen. In the scene he knocked around in, apart from stealing, there was only one way to get money. And that was something he couldn't come at. Now the thought of real money, for real work, almost blew his mind. His heart thumped like it had when he made his first grab and run. Again the thought, perhaps it *was* worth a try.

He didn't have to stay if he didn't like it. He looked up. 'I'll give it a go.'

Earl grinned. 'And I'll give you a go. Deal?' He reached across the table.

Bazza hesitated. This was a first. Self-consciousness slowed him. Then he gripped Earl's hand. He was surprised by its hardness. He was also touched by the friendly action. It made him feel ... perhaps not equal, but at least not the bottom of the heap.

Earl leaned back. 'Good. We'll start puttin' the pots in the water tomorrow. Right now, we better knock off these dishes, have a shower and hit the hay.'

'What time do you start?'

'We roll outta the sack around three ... half past.'

Bazza's eyebrows rocketed up. In the same instant he realised more visible emotion had escaped from him in these last few hours than he thought was possible. 'That's the middle of the night! How come?'

'To get as much done as possible before the screamin' southerly drives us round the bend. First good southerly, you'll know what I mean. Seems like the middle of the night but you'll get used to it.'

Bazza wiped the startled look from his face and settled it into its customary disgruntled, couldn't-care-less look. He stared at the table top. 'Find that hard to imagine.'

Earl grinned. 'You'll get used to lots of things. Like regular feeds and a bed. Where'd you sleep last night?'

'In the bush.'

'Cold?'

'Freezing.'

'Scared?'

Bazza's immediate reaction was to deny it, show he was tough. Then he shrugged, gave a lopsided grin. 'Stiff.' He then rushed on in an attempt to cover what he considered was an admission of weakness. 'Not used to the bush.'

Earl nodded, his expression non-judgemental. 'How about tucker?'

'Pinched it. Where and when I could.'

'Umm.' Earl rose to his feet. 'Time we knocked off these dishes. Then you better have a shower. Mind the water, it's hot.'

'How come you got hot water? Out here?'

'Two hundred litre drum at the back of the shed. Connected to a little overhead tank. Lit the fire under it this afternoon. We're on our own down here. Gotta do just about everything for ourselves.'

Bazza jerked awake. Fear iced his blood. He was scared. Where the hell was he? He was in a strange room. In a bed. The only light came from a torch lying on a bedside table. And someone was moving around!

His muscles tensed. How come he was in such a situation? The way to stay safe was to sleep rough, in dank out of the way spots. Hideaways existed in a city if you poked around enough. Old buildings, under bridges or subways, anywhere out of the wind. An old clothing bin. If you could get into it, and out again.

Then his memory jumped into gear. He recalled the previous day and his panic eased a little. He glanced at the window. It was black outside. He looked around. Saw Earl pull a thick woollen jumper over his shirt. His legs were bare below his shorts.

Bazza sat up. 'You weren't kiddin'?'

'Nope. It's three thirty.'

'How can we work in that?' Bazza gestured towards the window. Tiredness and aches crept back as the panic adrenalin dissipated.

'Be gettin' light by the time we've had breakfast.'

Bazza sat on the edge of the bed as Earl disappeared into the kitchen with the torch. Blackness engulfed him. Thoughts came together slowly. Probably because he'd slept more soundly than for a long time. Watch it, Bazz. Your defences have slipped.

What the hell *was* going on? He was in a warm comfortable bed for a change and that mad bugger wanted him to get up and work at some weird job that was done in the middle of the night! He glanced at the window. Take only seconds to disappear.

He placed his hand in the centre of the bed. The hollow was still warm from his body. Chill pimpled his skin and he was glad he hadn't slept in the open. Be a bastard to return to that so soon. Could take a blanket with him though. Get a grip on yourself, Bazz. Up and down, thoughts ran around in his head like Nintendo images in a video game.

A small engine started up. Light flooded the kitchen. It reminded Bazza of the previous evening when he sat beneath the fluorescent light and stuffed himself with the delicious stew the guy made. On second thoughts, if he pretended to go along with things, he could get some decent food into him.

Perhaps he should stick around for a while. Job couldn't be that bad.

He sidled into the kitchen area. A gas stove hissed blue flames beneath a frypan. Bacon sizzled its aroma into the room. A slice of bread crisped into toast on another burner. Bazza's interest quickened.

The breakfast was the best he'd eaten for ages. He started to come alive. It had been a long time since he'd had permission to sleep in a comfortable bed. Felt good — while it lasted. Probably be out on his ear once Earl tried him out as a decky. All he knew about fishing was that fish were supposed to like worms.

Outside, Bazza was surprised to see the night sky *was* lighter. Earl shut off the lighting plant, picked up a couple of oars and led him the short distance to the beach. A three metre aluminium dinghy sat on the sand above high water mark. They carried it to the water's edge. Bazza was surprised at its lightness.

Apprehensive about stepping into the dark water, Bazza stalled by trying to roll up his jeans. The legs were too tight. He gave up the attempt and joined Earl in lifting the dinghy. He pretended confidence and stepped into the water. It wasn't as cold as he expected. In fact it was warm compared to the air's early morning chill. When no mysterious creatures attacked him, he found he liked the feeling.

With the dinghy launched, Earl set up the oars and rowlocks and sat between them on the middle thwart. 'Shove us clear, Bazz, then step in and sit in the stern.' The boy hesitated. 'That's the blunt end,' Earl added.

Bazza thumped onto the stern thwart.

Earl started rowing. 'Ever rowed a dinghy, Bazz?'

'Nope.'

'Okay. Then watch and learn. Later, you can have a go. You'll soon pick it up.'

Earl pulled alongside the *Arium* and shipped the oars. He grabbed the dinghy's painter and climbed smoothly over the side of the larger boat. Swift movements tied the painter to the rail. He looked down at his new crewman. 'Your turn. Don't step on the side of the dinghy or you'll have an unexpected swim.'

About to do that, Bazza switched and scrambled awkwardly aboard. Earl moved to the wheelhouse and *Arium*'s engine roared into life. The sudden noise echoed from the limestone cliff and shattered the tranquillity of the bay. Bazza felt stunned and lost.

Earl lifted the spare anchor from the small hatch at the rear of the deck. It was shackled to a five metre length of chain and a strong nylon rope. He replaced the hatch, gathered up the anchor, chain and rope and moved for'ard. He indicated that Bazza should follow him.

On the foredeck, Earl showed him how to secure the rope to the mooring bit. 'Snug it' was the term he used. Bazza's first effort was messy. He persisted. Earl finally nodded. 'You've got it. Main thing is,

22

don't hurry. We're gunna do everything nice and easy to start with. Get the hang of things first, speed'll come later.' He dropped the mooring chain and swung back to the main deck. He engaged reverse. The prop bit into the water and dragged the stern towards the pots on the beach.

When it was still about fifty metres from the beach, he cut the throttle, leaned around the edge of the wheelhouse and called up to Bazza. 'Okay. Let her go!'

Bazza tossed over the spare anchor. Its chain clattered over the metal fairlead. The attached rope snaked after it, but soon slowed.

'Right. Now as I back in a bit closer, pay out the rope and snug it when I tell you.'

Bazza nodded.

A few minutes later Earl had the boat where he wanted it. He moved to the stern, grabbed a prepared length of rope and jumped over the side. He splashed into waist-deep water and waded ashore. He tethered the boat's stern to a star fence post driven deep into the beach, then waded back and shut off the engine.

'So far so good. Now comes the hard part. Put on one of those heavy waterproof aprons hangin' just inside the wheelhouse. It'll save your legs a bit.'

Again on shore, Earl hefted one of the batten craypots onto his shoulder and carried it out to the side of the boat. He put it on the steel rail topping the gunwale. 'Okay. Bazz, balance it there, slide it around the stern. Put it on the deck in that corner.'

Bazza was surprised by the pot's weight but soon got the hang of it. He paused when he arrived at the spot indicated by Earl. Earl cut in quickly. 'Don't lift it with your back bent. Lean back with it against your thighs. Use the leverage to balance it, move back a pace and lower the end onto the deck. Spot on. Lay three across like that. Then three more on top. We'll get four on the next row by leaning the outside ones on the rail. They'll angle in a bit.'

Bazza was glad Earl had advised him to wear the apron. By the time thirty pots and ropes were on board, he felt as though he'd been street mugged. Even his hands hurt from helping to tie on the ropes.

'That's enough for one trip. Besides, any more and we'll be sittin' on the bottom. Right, let's go.' Earl cast off the stern rope and restarted the engine. He indicated Bazza should move up onto the foredeck. 'Take in that rope as I ease forward.'

Sand swirled with the agitated water at the stern. It showed how close to the bottom the boat was. Bazza hauled the anchor on board as it moved forward. When there was sufficient water beneath the keel, Earl put the engine in neutral and showed him how to coil down the rope. 'You'll need to practice this. We do a lot of rope coiling in this game. Being able to do it quickly makes life a whole lot easier. And safer.' He stressed the last two words.

Earl headed towards the natural channel through the anchorage's protective reef. Once clear, he opened the throttle and headed seaward. 'We'll charge out a couple of miles and drop 'em in a line.' Earl put the boat onto the compass bearing he wanted.

Bazza picked up on the term 'miles'. 'Miles? Don't you mean kilometres?'

Earl nodded as he donned the other waterproof apron and tied the strings at his back. 'On land, yes. Distance at sea is measured in nautical miles. One nautical mile is equal to a minute of latitude. Or that's near enough for the moment. All navigation is based on it.'

'Oh!' Bazza's difficulty in absorbing the information came through in his voice.

Earl glanced at him. 'Sorry, Bazz. I'll dig out a chart, er map, and show you what I mean when we get ashore. Got a few charts of the area on board but a land map might make more sense to you at the moment.'

'Sure.' Bazza's bit of confidence over how he'd handled the pots and ropes quickly evaporated. Who was he kidding? Earl must think he was an idiot. Anyway, who cared? The way he hurt, he wasn't sure he wanted the job. Yeah, to hell with the bed and tucker, he'd split as soon as they got back to the beach.

Again Earl caught the despondent note in his voice and hastened to reassure him. 'You're doin' all right, Bazz. And don't be afraid to ask questions. Best way I know of learnin'. Sticks in the nut better.'

Bazza's nod was neutral. He jerked his head up as the back of the wheelhouse was licked with sunlight. He glanced astern and saw the sun nudge over the horizon. The sea began to sparkle. There was as yet no wind and he felt the peace of being away from the city's hassles.

He'd never watched the rising sun before. Of course he'd seen it, but it was just something that happened. This was different. Rich gold in colour, it was as yet not too bright to look at. He could actually see it moving. Seemed to mean something. Start of something perhaps?

Arriving in the area he wanted, Earl slowed the boat. 'I'll toss off the first one, then you have a go. I'll take it real slow.' He promptly lifted a pot from the stack and swung it onto the rail. Using his arms and the front of his thighs in unison, he shot the pot over the side. The rope followed, the floats flung wide and clear.

Bazza watched his every movement. 'Seems easy enough.'

'It is, if you keep your wits about you. Right, I'll keep an eye on you. If you get a rope snarled around your wrist or foot, brace yourself against the gunwale and hang on. I'll roar into reverse and belt back to help you. Okay?'

The dropping of the pots went slowly and without snarl-ups. Bazza knew he wasn't as smooth as his skipper but he felt a flush of achievement. Sure he fumbled a lot, but he got everything over in the right order. Panicked a few times, but coped.

Earl tied a marker buoy to the last pot rope and put it over the side. It had a long bamboo pole with a black and white flag at the top. 'Make it easier to spot the line when we come out again.' He opened the throttle and headed in for another load. 'So far so good. You're shaping up well, Bazza.'

Bazza was breathing heavily from the unusual exertion but there was also a strange tingle of inner warmth. He was used to abuse, not praise.

He'd been an embarrassment and an encumbrance to his mother. She played the field and a squalling brat had no place in her scheme of things.

Seedy day care centres and suspect 'baby sitters' came and went in a succession of painful experiences. School offered a chance. Hope stirred as true hearted people tried to help and teach him. Unfortunately, their efforts were doomed because his flighty mother never stayed in one place long enough for him to gain even the basics. As for his father? He was somewhere in that long line of come-and-go boyfriends.

Bazza leaned against the back of the wheelhouse. Perhaps he was more than a football for kicking? His breathing steadied as his body relaxed. Some of the muscle aches subsided. Jesus! That was hard work. Still, there was some satisfaction in knowing he'd taken part in a joint effort.

By the time they'd loaded and dropped another thirty pots, Bazza's muscles weren't grizzling, they were crying. Perspiration soaked his clothing and a single message hammered through his mind: this he didn't need. Earl was right when he said that would do for the day.

'Bring the last load tomorrow. Got a few things to sort out this afternoon.'

Bazza didn't answer: Okay. Earl, you sort 'em. Once we hit the shore, I'm off!

Back at the moorings, Bazza gaffed the rope between dinghy and mooring float. With Earl's assistance, he heaved up the heavy chain and dropped the looped end over the mooring bit. Bazza needed the help. He was stuffed. He put in only what he had to. Come on shore, I'm off!

'Before we go ashore, Bazz, I'll call the factory on the two-way and order the bait we'll need. I'll order some work clothes at the same time. What's your size?'

Bazza was startled by the request. The only clothes he had were the grotty ones he was wearing. They stank, but what could he do about it? It took a moment for his thoughts to regroup. 'Ummm … small men's I think. But I haven't got any money.'

'Makes two of us. By the start of the season I'm usually into the factory for a couple of thousand. A few more bucks isn't gunna make much difference.'

'Is that okay?'

'Without Mike Kailis's help, a lot of fishermen around here wouldn't have got started. Once we catch crays, some of the money we earn will be deducted until the loan is repaid. You'll pay for your clothes that way. Or anything else you need.'

Bazza was stunned. It was an entirely new concept. For a second he forgot his hurts. Did that make him *real*? He groped for something to cover his runaway thoughts. 'Er … how long's the closed season?'

'Three months. Long time with nothin' comin' in. With so much goin' out on maintenance and gear, it's a bit of a scratch around now. Take on the odd job when one crops up. Helps. And that reminds me, must ask the guy at the factory to keep an ear to the ground. Be handy if a job came up during one of our slack periods.'

'Is it always like that?'

'Another couple of years and my boat'll be paid for. Then, with a bit of luck, I'll have some in the kitty to tide me over. I won't have to go into debt.'

'Sounds tough.'

'Gettin' better each year. Scored a job with the Fisheries earlier this closed season.'

'Doin' what?'

'Carted some artificial cray shelters out. They wanted to run trials on 'em. We dumped 'em a couple of miles out. Job lasted ten days.'

'Get many jobs like that?'

''Fraid not. The odd night trip fishin' for dhufish helps. Can't spend too much time at it though. Gotta overhaul the boat and get the gear ready.'

'Sounds like a lotta hard work.'

'Wouldn't swap places with any of those tycoons in Perth. They're forever runnin' around like blue arsed flies gettin' ulcers on their ulcers. I've got a bed and a feed. And I'm my own boss. I like what I'm doin'. What more could any man want? Besides less wind and more money?'

Bazza joined in laughing, but didn't really know what Earl was on about.

'Right, I'll call the factory then we'll go ashore and get some tucker into us.'

Bazza's intention of doing a runner receded as he untied the dinghy from the rope on the mooring chain. Right then, a feed sounded like a damned good idea. He led the dinghy alongside. He wasn't sure what Earl meant about less wind. At the moment, the light sea-breeze was a relief from the heat. Where was the problem?

Earl suggested Bazza should get into the middle of the dinghy and try his hand at rowing. Bazza nodded, why not? Looked easy enough. Even his tired muscles could handle that. He climbed down and sat on the middle thwart. He set up the oars and rowlocks as he'd seen Earl do in the semi-darkness of the early morning.

Earl pushed the dinghy clear of *Arium* and sat back. The ball was in Bazza's court. He made a mess at first but soon got the hang of it and snake tracked to the beach. They carried the dinghy to above high water mark.

Bazza forced his body to haul himself up the

beach. Right then he doubted he could run anywhere. First things first. A feed and sit down. After that … he'd play it by ear.

Bazza dawdled along the water's edge. It was mid-afternoon. He wore a pair of Earl's khaki shorts, held up by a length of nylon cord. His own freshly washed clothes flapped with some of Earl's on the line at the back of the shack. Earl had gone to talk to some fishermen who had shacks at the northern end of the limestone 'cliff'. Bazza shied off accompanying him. Dodging people was a hard habit to break. Earl hadn't pushed the point but suggested he might like to walk south along the deserted beach.

Bazza was tired and sore. Even his hands hurt, but a refreshing shower and feed had made him temporarily drop his plan to run. Had his luck changed? Naagh, watch it Bazz. Don't get carried away. Since when was luck your mate? In the past every time he'd thought things were getting better, he'd received a kick in the guts. For instance, the time the guy from that church group 'helped' him. Like Earl, he offered him a bed, a feed and a shower. Even supplied him clean second-hand clothes. Then, he'd crowded him. Wanted to touch him all the time. When he joined him in the shower cubicle, Bazza kicked him where it hurt and lit out for the other end of town.

Earl hadn't crowded him, but there were similarities. True, he offered these things in return for work.

He told him he'd pay for his own clothes and tucker once they earned some hard cash. Bazza liked the sound of that. Hand-outs in the past had strings attached. Maybe this set up *was* different. Maybe. His street cunning again told him to watch it. He'd see which way the wind blew.

Thoughts of the wind made him study his surroundings. He liked the space. Nothing threatened. The sea-breeze was now quite strong, and looking seaward, he saw caps of froth charging down the slopes of waves that were everywhere he looked. He wondered what it would be like out on the boat.

However, despite the wind, the sun was hot on Bazza's bare torso. He looked at the water. Glances in both directions showed nothing but deserted beach. He dropped his shorts on the sand. A couple of bounds and he was knee deep. He dived into crystal clear water. After the shock of the coolness, and a burst of vigorous swimming, he relaxed and luxuriated in the warmer water close to the shore. His hurts eased further.

As he lay there looking at the empty beach, he realised what Earl meant about not swapping places with anyone in the city. Bazza would never return to living like a sewer rat. He was out and he'd do his damnedest to stay out. Let the creepy bastards stay in their own dung heap. If any ventured up here, which seemed unlikely, at least he'd see 'em coming.

Even as he thought that, he realised he had decided to stay. At least for the present. Thoughts of the evening meal coming up, with a soft bed to follow, sounded better than a night shivering under a bush with an empty belly.

Over the next week he found out about the wind. Sometimes the sea-breeze was blowing even before they stepped on board. Other times it didn't arrive until mid-morning or even later. The later it came, the easier their job was. Light winds were okay. Screaming southerlies or beasterly easterlies were a pain in the butt.

Pulling and baiting the pots was an unforgettable experience. It made him wonder again what the hell he was doing there. Bait smells turned his stomach. Earl told him not to think about it but concentrate on the job in hand. It was sound advice. The motion of the boat also took some getting used to, but so far, he'd only 'chuckled' over the side a couple of times. Even his muscles no longer hurt as much.

How Earl knew where to drop the pots was a mystery to Bazza. Or how he found them again the next day. Sure the compass and echo sounder played their part, and he noticed Earl lining up landmarks on the shore, but the crays weren't everywhere. Miss the good ground and you got nothing.

For the first few days of the season they caught only a handful of crays. Then cracked a bag. To use Earl's words: the whites had started. With a bit of luck they should have a good run for a few weeks before the crays left the shallows and headed out. Earl admitted he hadn't been successful in the really deep water. As a result, he chose to burn less fuel and stick to where he did know how to catch the critters. When the whites did cut out, and after a lull of a few weeks, the reds would start in the shallows. The run was less dramatic but it continued for the rest of the season.

Bazza was glad Earl had made that decision in the past. He'd already noticed the further out you went, the bigger the waves. Big waves made the work harder.

Day by day, Bazza slid more easily into the accepting niche. He wasn't exactly in love with the work but he liked the comforts, like a bed and feeds. For the moment he was prepared to put up with one to gain the other. Hot showers were sheer luxury.

'Ah! That's better.' Earl's hair was wet from the shower and freshly combed as he stepped from the bathroom. He smelled better too. He wore black shorts and his brown torso was bare, as were his feet. It was always a relief to get rid of the accumulation of smells from a day's pot pulling. Salt, disturbed sea bottom and bits of decayed bait sprayed them when a pot slammed up onto the tipper. Dehydrated by sun and wind, it made the skin feel like bootleather. 'Your turn, Bazz.'

Perched on the edge of a chair, Bazza was still covered in his layer of gunk. It was crusted on his face, arms and legs. Curved white lines of salt on his shirt and shorts showed where water had been dried by sun and wind. Ironically, the cause of the damage had now dropped. Outside it was warm and still with the sea looking as innocent as a babe. No wonder Earl called that wind a 'beasterly easterly.' Bazza could think of stronger words.

'Hate that easterly. Thought I hated the southerly but I've changed my mind.'

Earl grinned. 'You and me both. All winds are a nuisance in this game but that one takes the cake. It whips up a short sharp chop. Boat doesn't get time to climb over one wave before it's slap bang into the next. And the next. And the next.'

'How about tomorrow?'

'More of the same I should think.'

'Blast!' Bazza respected Earl's judgement when it came to the weather. Something every fisherman learnt quickly. He forced his tired body from the chair and headed for the shower. 'Oh, well. Be nice to get rid of the gunk for a while.' He didn't bother to shut the bathroom door. For the first few days he'd kept a watchful eye on it but now knew there was nothing to fear. Earl was as straight as they came.

Water came from rain water tanks and was thus limited, but once you learned the technique, you didn't need much to have a good shower. Wet yourself, turn off the water, then soap yourself all over before sluicing down again. Bazza quickly got the hang of it and there was no doubt about it, rain water left you squeaky clean. He liked the feeling. Sleeping and fending rough no longer appealed.

As Bazza disappeared, Earl settled into a bean bag. He reflected on how well the lad was shaping up. His gamble appeared to be working. If he could get the kid interested, he might stay for an extended period. Do them both a favour.

Bazza was young, but under his belligerent mask of indifference, he was willing. Earl smiled. Reminded him of himself. No great shakes as a scholar, he'd quit school as soon as he got a job as a decky. He'd had a hard skipper and crayfishing was a tough game. You either liked it or hated it. Earl saw past the abuse dished out by his skipper and liked it. He also believed you didn't need to be a bastard to get the best out of your crew.

Today, they'd got nearly seven bags. The whites had probably peaked in their area. It would undoubtedly be of short duration in the shallows, but what the hell? They'd make the most of it while they lasted. The mad frenetic guessing game of where, and if, the whites would run, was over. They'd kicked off nicely. At the end of the week there would be a decent sized cheque to collect.

The approach into his shack, once clear of the limestone, was simply two sandy wheel tracks. The truckie who picked up the fishermen's catch each day knew how to handle them. He dropped off bait and supplies on his way south and returned an hour or so later to pick up Earl's neat stack of bags.

Picking up other fishermen's catches on the way, the truck would be loaded by the time he returned to the factory at Dongara.

Earl let the feeling of having finished the day's work float over him. In an hour or so he'd rouse himself and cook the evening meal. Meanwhile, it was relax time.

It was a hot summer's day. If the sea-breeze came, it would be late and weak. Earl got a couple of cold drinks from the fridge, one for himself and one for Bazza, and settled in the coolest part of the shack. They'd already knocked up and eaten a belated lunch. When they got in, food was always their first priority. Earl smiled to himself. It still gave him pleasure to see how the kid tucked into his food.

A noise came from the adjoining shed. What was Bazza was doing out there? Be like an oven in there now.

He suddenly sat up. Bazza was in the shower. He could hear the water running.

Earl rolled to his feet. Strange, he hadn't heard a vehicle. He moved to the doorway. The track in was empty. The noise came again. Metal clinked on metal. It definitely came from the shed.

He walked out into the sun. Heat fell on him. The sand was fast-footwork hot. His feet made no sound as he approached the open front of the shed. His white Holden was parked inside. In such an isolated spot, Earl removed the keys but seldom locked the vehicle.

Movement caught his eye. The driver's side door was open. An intruder knelt on the ground as he fiddled with the wires beneath the dash.

'Hey! What the hell're you doin'?' Earl surged forward.

A second man stepped out from in front of the ute. The rifle in his hands was pointed at Earl's chest.

'Hold it Buster!' The man was about ten years older than Earl. Perspiration beaded and trickled, dripped off his nose and chin. He looked as though he'd walked a long way in the heat. He looked mean. He spoke to his mate in the cab. 'Relax, Ray. Buster here's gunna give us his keys.'

'Like hell I will!' Earl's anger peaked. He'd worked damned hard for what he had. He took a step forward.

The safety catch snicked off. It sounded loud and threatening in the shed. Earl stopped. The weapon was beyond reach and the business end of a rifle looks nasty at the best of times. It looks worse when it's pointed at your chest.

'Back off!' Hard man gestured with the rifle.

Earl backed from the shed. He squashed his anger. It was time to use his head.

Ray got out of the cab. He was about Earl's age. He held out his hand. 'Gimme!'

'Haven't got 'em.'

'Where are they?'

Earl jerked his head towards the shack. 'Inside.'

'Then you better get 'em hadn't you?' Hard man's voice sounded as hard as he looked. 'We'll be right behind you.' He patted the rifle stock where it rested against his hip. His meaning was plain.

Earl turned and walked the short distance to the shack. His feet were tough from working barefooted but even so he was glad to get off the hot sand. The two men crowded in behind him, watching, ready to react if he made a sudden movement.

Bazza came out of the bathroom.

Ray snapped a warning. 'Look out, Ken! There's another one!'

So, hard man's name was Ken. Earl made the mental note in the moment before Ken jabbed him just below his left shoulder. The rifle muzzle hurt. Earl lurched forward and almost collided with Bazza. He spun quickly but Ken had them both covered. The movement had brought the two fishermen together. Ken kept his eyes on them as he spoke to Ray. 'Grab some food outta the fridge.'

Bazza recognised them as the men who nearly trapped him in the shack down the coast. The memory of the hungry days that followed still rankled. And dammit! Here they were doing it again. He felt a sudden surge of anger. This was his and Earl's food, bought and paid for with their own hard work! He started forward. 'Hang on! That's all we've got 'till the truck brings our next order!'

Earl stopped him. He spoke softly but urgently. 'Easy, Bazz …'

'Listen to your mate, Sonny Boy. That way you won't get holes in ya. And you, Buster, where're the keys?'

Earl nodded towards the fridge. 'On top.' A worm of blood crawled down his back. The rifle jab had broken the skin. Cold anger spread through him. Its very slowness enabled him to think productively.

Ray, busy poking food into a plastic bag, stopped

and looked up. He spotted the keys, grabbed and pocketed them. He resumed his ransacking.

Ken's impatience showed in the tightness around his mouth. Earl guessed that now he had a vehicle, he wanted to get the hell out of the area. Probably felt they'd already been around too long. 'That'll do, Ray. Let's get outta here.'

'Not much petrol in the ute.'

Bazza glanced at Earl. Why tell 'em?

Ken suspected a trick of some sort. He aimed the rifle at Earl's chest. 'Then fill it! Where d'ya keep your supply?'

'Drum behind the shed.'

'How do you get it into the ute?'

'Hand pump.'

'That's what I like, a bit of co-operation. Now, how about a bit more. Ray, drive the ute around to the back of the shed. Buster here is gunna fill it.'

Ray hefted the plastic bag of food and went out the door. He didn't bother to shut the fridge. Ken indicated with the rifle. Earl and Bazza followed. They stepped into their rubber thongs as they went out.

Unsettling thoughts flicked through Bazza's mind. If he hadn't bumped into Earl, he'd have ended up like this. They were on the merry-go-round. Where things only got worse. Older kids sometimes got fed up and moved into the big time. Those not already in prison wouldn't stop until they killed someone. Or got themselves killed. He knew it was damned hard to get off. Earl had given him the chance.

But what had happened to his skipper? He'd gone to water. He was bending over backwards to help these guys. They'd rob him blind. Bazza's confusion grew as Ken herded them.

Behind the shed, Earl positioned himself between the fuel and the watchful Ken. He unscrewed the bung of the two hundred litre drum of lighting kerosense he used to fill the fridge. He inserted the rotary pump and uncoiled its hose. Ray stopped the ute alongside and got out of the cab. Earl undid the cap on the ute's fuel tank and poked in the nozzle.

Ray shoved him aside before he started pumping. 'Smart arse!' he snarled. 'Think I can't read? Or smell?'

Earl regained his balance and looked at the top of the drum. 'Oh! Sorry, mate. You guys have got me rattled.' He moved to the next drum and unscrewed its bung. Ray made sure he didn't step between Ken and Earl as he checked. It was petrol. Dubious about the excuse, he kept his mouth shut as Earl worked on the pump. Ken trained the rifle on the fishermen. The muzzle drifted from one to the other.

Still pumping, Earl looked down and nudged the tyre alongside him with his foot. 'Bit puddeny. Should've pumped 'em up earlier. Just haven't got round to it. Don't go to town much. Likely to blow a tyre like that. Maybe several on a long trip.'

Ken flicked a glance at the tyres. Then back. His hard glare never left the men for long. One glance was enough. The tyres bulged markedly. 'Got a pump?'

'Small compressor.' Earl felt Bazza's gaze. Sensed what he was thinking. He kept his eyes from the boy's face and continued pumping.

'Where is it?'

'In the shed. I'll get it.'

Bazza cringed. Jesus! What was he up to? He'd be belly up like a pup before long.

Ken had different thoughts. 'Like hell you will. Ray! Get the compressor.'

Ray scurried around into the shed. He found the petrol driven compressor. It was heavy. He grunted as he lifted it. It banged against his thighs as he waddled back. He plonked it on the sand at the rear of the ute.

'Bit tricky to start. I'll do it if you like.' Earl started to move from the drum.

'Hold it!' Ken spat the command like a broken tooth. 'Think I came down in the last shower? You two stay together. Fill the ute, then fix the tyres.'

Fuel gurgled in the throat of the tank. Earl stopped pumping and withdrew the end of the hose. He casually turned back to the drum. As though by accident, his thumb half covered the nozzle of the hose. It was directed at Ken. His other hand was still on the pump handle where it had come to rest at the top of its circle.

The rifle spat. The blast stunned Earl as the bullet screamed past his head.

'Don't even think about it!'

Earl's left ear buzzed. Ken's words came as though from a distance. Even so, he couldn't miss the menace in it. He flexed his jaw to clear his ear and let his senses regroup. He started to remove the pump from the drum.

'Leave it!' Ken snapped. 'Fix the tyres.' He jerked the rifle barrel in the direction he wanted them to go. His meaning was clear.

Earl started the compressor and waited a few moments for the tank to build pressure. He then filled the tyres. Using his eyes as a gauge, he stopped when each tyre was upright and taut. Finally he shut off the compressor.

Ken motioned the fishermen back against the wall. 'If I were you, I'd stay there for a while. We're heading south. Which track's the best one to take?'

'Why should I tell you?'

Ken moved the rifle. 'Because, Buster, we've got nothing to lose. You have. Got it?'

Earl hesitated and Bazza thought he was at last going to show some spirit. His disgust returned when Earl pointed with his chin towards the beach. 'Tide's low with these easterlies. Bore along the hard sand at the edge and you'll miss the traffic on the other road. The truckie, and fishermen from further down the coast'll be headin' up to Dongara about now. Some of 'em are a bit lead footed. It's mostly a one vehicle track and a lot of the corners are blind.'

'What kind of bum steer are you giving us now?'

Ken looked angry. His actions with the rifle more menacing.

'Hope to eventually get my ute back. When you've finished with it. In roughly the same shape as now, not scrunched against the roobar of a Landrover with blood splattered all over the inside.'

Ken grunted. He nudged his companion towards the ute. 'You heard him.'

Ray got in and started the engine. As the ute moved, Ken slid into the passenger's seat. The Holden rolled towards the beach, made it to the hard sand and roared off. It disappeared around the small headland to the south.

'Bastards!' Bazza spat. 'There goes your ute!' Past experiences flashed through his mind. Some he'd taken part in, some he'd only heard about. 'Bastards'll torch it when they dump it. How're you gunna get another one? We'll be stuck here.' Then the irony of his feelings struck him. When you had nothing, you had nothing to lose. He still didn't have much but was stunned to realise he valued his changed circumstances. Strange emotions stirred.

Earl was slow in answering, his gaze on the sand at his feet. He appeared to be deep in thought. When he raised his hand slightly, Bazza realised he was listening. He shut his mouth and waited.

Earl finally grunted. 'Maybe.'

Bazza could contain himself no longer. 'Did you have to help 'em so much?'

'Can't help anyone, least of all yourself, with a bullet hole in your chest.'

Bazza agreed with that. 'Yeah. Still ... what're we gunna do now?'

'Let's go out to the boat.'

Bazza was surprised but after a moment he shrugged and followed Earl to the beach. He hoped he knew what he was doing.

Arium's anchor chain was vertical. Only the occasional catspaw rippled the anchorage. Outside the reef, the sea was flat calm.

'Wouldn't you know it,' Bazza grumbled. 'Easterly beats the hell outta us while we're working, then when we've finished, it pisses off.'

Earl grinned. 'No one tells the weather man what to do.'

Bazza trailed the dinghy from the stern as Earl moved into the wheelhouse and switched on the two-way.

Traffic was thin on the air. He didn't have long to wait.

'6DI, 6DI, 6DI. This is *Arium* calling. Do you read me? Over.'

'DI to *Arium*. Go ahead Earl.'

'Are there two crims on the run?'

'Er … that rings a bell. Yeah, police alerted us a few weeks ago. Seen 'em?'

'Think so.'

There was a pause, then the Dongara factory came back on air. 'Sorry for the delay … dug out some info. Right. One middle-aged, one younger. Broke out of Greenough Prison early November.'

'First names Ken and Ray?'

'Yes. Police consider them dangerous but not armed.'

'They are now. Picked up a rifle somewhere.'

'And ammunition?'

'Goes bang.'

'You okay?'

'Yep.'

'Know where they are now?'

'Heading south. Probably on foot by now.' Earl heard Bazza's sharp intake of breath.

'How long since they left?'

'Ten minutes or so.'

'Right. I'll pass that onto the police. Put the cat among the pigeons I reckon. Everyone thought they'd left the area. Thanks for the info. Out.'

'Hang on! Before you go. How about sending some tucker on tomorrow's truck?'

'Roger. What do you want?'

'Usual weekly order.'

'So soon? Must be hungry this week.'

'Made an unexpected donation.'

'Ah! Okay. Out.'

Earl cradled the mike and switched off the two-way. Bazza couldn't contain himself.

'Why tell 'em they're on foot. They'll be kilometres away by now. Coast down there goes on forever. Apart from fishermen's shacks, there's nothin'. Believe me, I've been there. It's nowhere. You'd need an army to find anyone. It's a bum lead. Cops'll be fumin'. That won't break my heart, but you'll never get your ute back!'

'We'll see.'

'Jeez! How can you be so calm? We've got nothin' to eat tonight!' Even as he said it, he remembered plenty of nights when he'd eaten nothing. He liked his present situation and didn't want it disturbed.

Earl tried to allay his distress. 'Hey! We're fishermen aren't we?' He indicated the sea. 'We'll catch a fish.'

Bazza looked at him in surprise for a moment. Yes! He was no longer a victim of how life kicked him. He *could* do something to help himself. He felt a surge of thanks and growing affection for the man standing in front of him. To cover his 'softness', he pretended a grudging agreement. 'Hell, I give in. Okay. Let's go catch a fish.'

'Let's go for a walk first.'

Bazza rolled his eyes skyward. 'Yeah, why not? Let's pick some flowers while we're at it.'

Earl grinned and playfully punched Bazza on the

arm. 'Hang in there, Bazz. I think I know what I'm doing.'

The fishermen beached the dinghy and walked to the shack. Bazza followed. He was sure his skipper had flipped.

Earl got a plastic bottle of water that had been left in the fridge. The men who'd stolen the rest of the fridge's contents would regret leaving that behind before the day was finished. He picked up a battered cloth hat and indicated Bazza should do the same. 'Be hot walkin' now the wind's dropped.'

They returned to the beach and walked south. The vehicle's tracks were imprinted in the sand. Except where a larger than usual swell had driven a beach wave up the slight slope and wiped the slate clean.

They walked about two kilometres before they spotted Earl's ute in the bite of a small bay. Trying to skirt a metre high build up of flotsam and seaweed, it was bogged in loose sand. There was no sign of Ken and Ray.

Earl and Bazza found the ute undamaged, except for a new dent in the driver's side door. Looked as though a boot had been planted there. Sand at the back of the tailgate was heavily scored by someone trying to push the ute through. Footprints angled across the windswept beach and disappeared over the first sandhill.

Earl walked at right angles to the beach to where tough beach scrub struggled against wind and sea.

He searched among the scruffy branches.

Jesus, Bazza thought, he really is gunna look for flowers. He was slightly mollified when he saw his skipper break off a small twig. When Earl broke it in two and handed one piece to him, he again wondered. Hell of a time to pick your teeth.

'Start lettin' down the tyres. We want 'em nice and puddeny. Like they were before I pumped 'em up.' Earl glanced at how deeply the tyres had churned into the sand. 'Maybe a bit more.'

Still puzzled, Bazza squatted by the nearest tyre. Hisses of air broke the stillness. Hot rubber smells overrode the beach odours.

It didn't take long. When Earl was satisfied with the pudginess of the tyres, he knelt beside one rear wheel and scooped sand from the back of it. Bazza did the same on the other side. When the sand sloped behind each wheel, and the diff, Earl got into the driver's seat and started the engine. He looked at Bazza. 'Mind givin' us a push on the front?'

Bazza did so. Earl engaged reverse and let out the clutch. He kept the revs low and the flattened tyres grabbed at the sand and wound up out of their holes. He reversed until the ute was clear of the deep, soft sand and on the hard strip by the water's edge. He then stopped and opened the passenger's door. 'Hop in.'

Bazza was happy to do so. He'd quit pushing as soon as the ute reached the packed sand. Even that short spell was hot, hard work. He accepted the bottle of water Earl offered him and drank thirstily. A thought flashed into his mind as he lowered the bottle. The cunning bastard!

Earl turned for home. 'Right. Now let's go catch that fish.'

Over the next couple of days they settled back into their routine. The third day brought an early fresh sea-breeze and they took a hiding. Both were glad to be back on shore and wrapping themselves around a late lunch.

Earl finally pushed his plate away. 'Aaah! That's more like it. Backbone was rubbin' a hole in me.'

Bazza finished on a slab of bread and jam. 'You and me both.' He cocked his head as a stronger gust rattled the door. Something banged against the wall. 'Another reason I'm glad we've finished. Wind was gettin' a bit unfriendly on that last line. Got a sneaky habit of chuckin' water over ya when you're not lookin'.'

Earl grinned and nodded. 'According to the weather report, there's a weak cold front heading for the south-west corner of the state. Bit early for winter patterns. Doubt we'll get much up here but it could bring some swell.'

'That good?'

'Should be. A stir-up makes the crays crawl. Maybe it disturbs their natural tucker and they sneak up on it in the murk.'

'Goin' out tomorrow?'

'Bloody oath! Never miss a day if you can help it. Learnt that early in the piece, just after I got my first boat.'

'First?'

'Yeah. Smaller and slower. Fished from Dongara then. I can remember mornings when I've stood on the beach with some of the other fishermen and discussed whether or not to go out. A few of the guys used to point to the horizon and say, 'Look at those bumps. Big swell out there. Be rough as guts.' I used to get sucked in until an old fisherman, Karl Ricks, told me to ignore the no-hopers and get on out there.'

'You take his advice?'

'Yep. Best thing I ever did. Took some hidings from the sea but Karl was dead right. It pays to keep your pots clean and freshly baited. "Pull 'em as regularly as you can," he used to say. "Chuck out all the old bones and sucked out cray shells." Gave me some good tips in those early days. Most of all, "Don't think you can be lazy just because you're your own boss." He also told me, to be successful at anything, you must have good gear. That's why I stuck my neck out and went for the *Arium*.'

'You work for him once?'

'Nope, he's a loner.'

'What made him give you advice then?'

Earl thought for a moment. 'Dunno. Seemed to take a shine to me. Bit like a Dutch Uncle.'

'What's a Dutch Uncle.'

'Umm … someone who gives you advice without pullin' any punches. Cranky old bugger, used to lay it on pretty thick, but his advice was good.'

Another wind gust shook the shack. Earl met Bazza's look. The latter's eyebrows rose. 'A weak front?'

Earl smiled. 'Fear not. This shack can stand a lot worse than that.'

'You sure?'

'My reputation as a builder stands on it.'

'What reputation?'

'I'm known all over this town.'

'Population seven?'

Earl grinned as another gust rolled a metal bucket past the back of the shed. 'Sounds like an afternoon for me to get some paperwork done.'

'What sort of paperwork?'

'Fisheries returns for the month.'

'That what you call red tape?'

'Guess so. Never thought I'd be doin' it.'

'Why are you?'

'Have to if I wanna keep fishin'.'

'And you want to?'

Earl's nod was emphatic. 'Badly enough to learn how. Couldn't read and write a spit, and couldn't care less, until I found I had to. No read and write, no skipper's ticket.'

'Fishin' that important to you?'

'Sure is!' Earl thought a moment before answering

more fully. 'It's something I can do reasonably well. I'm not kiddin' myself I'm a crash hot fisherman, but … um, can't quite explain it but it makes me feel … useful.'

Bazza thoughtfully digested the information. A few weeks ago he wouldn't have known what Earl was talking about. Now he did.

Earl started to clear the table. 'What're you gunna do this arvo, after we've done the dishes?' he added pointedly.

Bazza looked resigned and got to his feet. 'Dunno. Haven't thought about it.'

Earl indicated a makeshift cupboard that doubled as a bookcase. 'Some magazines there. Be a few comics kickin' around. Used to be a Phantom fan.'

After a few moments, Bazza pushed out the words. 'Can't read.' The tone was flat, with an edge of belligerence.

Earl showed little surprise. 'Not at all?'

The query hit a sore spot and Bazza prickled. 'What if I don't? Stuff the readin'.'

'Hey! I'm not knockin' ya. I muddled through school without much rubbin' off on me. Reckon you learn more out of school than in it. Least I did.' Earl was thoughtful a moment. 'Guess you learn when you want to.'

'Bein' dragged around by my old woman, I went to more schools than there are rubbish dumps. Hated 'em all.'

'Not to worry.' Earl gathered some jars and put

them back in the fridge. Bazza collected the dishes and put them on the sink. Most of the jobs got done between them without any spoken decision as to who did what.

Earl tossed in a suggestion. 'Why not go for a walk along the beach. Even though it's blowin', if you rug up well you'll probably enjoy it.'

'What's there to do on a beach in this?' Bazza jerked a thumb at the sound of the wind outside.

'Just look. And feel. Sure it's no place for swimmin' at the moment, but you'll see it in a different light. Good place for thinkin'.'

Bazza nodded. Might as well.

Earl had almost finished his paperwork when he heard a vehicle stop outside the shack. He put down his biro, got to his feet, walked to the door and pushed it open against the wind.

Two men got out of a Landrover.

Bazza was returning from his walk. Earl was right, the beach was different when it turned wintry. The sea had changed. The waves were angry and the water was stirred. It was discoloured with sand and floating stuff swirled from the bottom. A mauve coloured sea urchin rolled up the beach but managed to retain most of its spikes. Strange looking seaweed washed ashore. A floppy sea animal oozed purple ink onto the sand when he turned it over. Seabirds were unfazed by the blustery wind. They zoomed around as though it blew especially for them.

He crunched up the small sandhill. As his head came level with the crest he glanced towards the shack. And froze. He knew a cop car when he saw one. 'Cops' was written all over the two men walking towards the house. He crouched. His heart hammered and he looked at the beach behind him. Which way should he run? Were the cops travelling north or south?

He cautiously lifted his head and saw the bulky men approach Earl. Earl made inviting-in gestures and stepped out to hold the door in the wind that blew away the sounds of their voices. The two men entered and Earl followed them inside, holding the door firmly until it closed.

Bazza dropped below the crest. Jesus! Here it was again. Bent over, he scurried down onto the beach and walked north along the water's edge. He kicked savagely at a straggle of weed.

The last time he was picked up, he'd lashed out and got roughed up for his trouble. After a couple of days in the cooler, the magistrate warned him: 'Next time you will get a stint of "detainment" in something tougher than a reha-bilitation centre. People like you need to be made an example of.'

The irony was, on that particular break-in, he'd taken only food. The easiest loot to dispose of. You ate it. Unfortunately, the owner of the house was a man of authority and substance. He pulled no punches in pressing charges. Must have considered

Bazza a threat to his importance and standing in his little pumped-up world.

Bastard was right about one thing. Unless he was stopped, he, Bazza, would inevitably slide back into his own muck heap. Bazza could feel himself sliding. How the hell could you get right off?

Snug in the shack, the senior policeman lowered a half empty mug to the table top. Steam wisped from the rim of the mug. His companion folded a sheet of paper. Earl's signature was on the bottom.

'Ah! That hit the spot. Bitch of a day.'

Earl nodded. 'Where did you catch up with 'em?'

'Bout ten ks down the coast. They'd made pretty good time.'

'Still have the rifle?'

'Yeah. Threatened a lot but eventually put it down. Convinced them there were police closing on them from the east and south. And the heat had got to them. Tongues were hanging out for a drink. Had a couple of days to cool off since then.'

'Sure glad you got 'em. Bit too free with that rifle for my likin'.'

'Thanks for the tip. Led us right to them. Been

giving us the run-around for a while. I thought they'd done a flit. Left the state maybe. Must've hung around after a vehicle. Not many around before the season started. We've got your statement but we'll need you as a witness later. Let you know when.'

'Okay.'

'Steal anything else, besides your ute?'

'Bit of tucker.'

The policeman nodded. 'Reports filtered in after the fishermen returned to their shacks. Malicious damage but mostly just tinned food, beds slept in. That sort of stuff.' He paused a moment. 'Funny thing is, there were two distinct types of break-ins.' He looked directly at Earl. 'Have any other unwelcome visitors?'

Bazza slowed. Finally stopped. Stared at the wet sand by his feet. His 'seeing' was all in his mind. Mostly pictures of abusive situations. Abuse at 'home', abuse in remand centres. Even abuse in so called havens for homeless kids. Maybe they weren't all like that, but if so, he'd failed to find one that wasn't. What was the matter with him? Was there a big ABUSE ME sign draped around his neck or something? Was that all there was to life? Bashings and beltings until you laid down and died?

He believed so, until he ran into Earl. Things changed then. Or was he just in a calm spell? A calm spell now ended? Was he destined to always be in the rough?

Where could he go? From trips to Dongara and Geraldton with Earl, he knew there were no shacks north of Cliffhead. If he hung around Dongara, he'd stick out like a sore thumb. Might get lost in Geraldton. Maybe get a job on another crayboat. Naagh. If the cops were after him, it wouldn't take them long to locate a newcomer, particularly one late on the scene.

Head south? There were shacks that way, but they would now be occupied. Even if he only stole food, word would soon get around via the two-way.

Head inland? There were farms in there some-where. Maybe he could get a job on one of them. Same problem. Word would get around. Strange kids didn't knock on farmhouse doors looking for work.

Damn! What the hell could he do? He lifted his head and stared at the line of sandhills. Miserable country! Covered in rubbishy bits of scrub that looked like he felt, battered and bashed by every strong breeze that came along. If the salt didn't kill them, the gales did.

Suddenly, his focus shifted. The bushes weren't beaten, they'd adapted! The business with the two cons returned in full detail. If Earl had stood up against them, they'd have smashed him flat. Instead, he bent, survived, and beat them. Again the thought, the cunning bastard!

Bazza turned and walked back towards Cliffhead. When he reached the anchorage, he paused before walking over the crest of the sandhill. He was scared. Then he swore. To hell with 'em! He would bend and survive. Nothing could smash him flat!

He stared over the crest at the shack. The Landrover had gone. A temporary reprieve? He squared his shoulders, took a deep breath and walked on.

He pulled open the door and looked quickly around. Earl lolled in a bean bag, a magazine in his hands. Bazza shut the door. His hair was wind blown, his face red and cold. Sullenness returned to his voice. 'What'd the cops want?'

'To thank us for leading them to those two cons. Wanted a statement, and I'll be needed as a witness at their trial.'

'Caught 'em then?'

'Yep. Bit hot and bothered. The coast south of here can be a mite unfriendly when you're hoofin' it on a hot day.'

'Tell me about it.'

Earl looked at him. Bazza's defensive mask was back in place. 'Fill a bean bag, Bazz. We've got the afternoon off, remember.'

'Think I should move on.' Bazza made no move to relax or sit down.

'Got anywhere to go?'

'Nope.'

'Then do me a favour. Stay here.'

'Gotta go.'

'Not in my book.' Earl pushed the bean bag closer

to Bazza's feet. 'Take the weight off.'

Bazza hesitated, then flopped into the bag. 'They ask about me?' His voice was tight, as though he was reluctant to ask.

'Not 'specially. Mentioned some break-ins down the coast.'

'Comin' back?'

'Doubt it. Told 'em someone knocked off a bit of tucker when I was out on the boat. Never saw 'em. Suggested whoever it was must've continued on up the coast.'

The two became silent. Bazza hands were clasped between his knees as he stared at the wall. Relief calmed his pumped-up emotions. He croaked one word. 'Thanks.'

Earl looked at him. When he spoke his tone was easy. 'We're helpin' each other, Bazz. You're shaping up well. We're a good team. Why muck that up with you goin' on an enforced holiday? Besides, I need you.'

Bazza's head jerked up. Their glances met and held. Then he dropped his head and stared at his feet. He was stunned. This was something new. Needed! The thought almost blew his mind. New emotions ran amuck and he didn't know what to do. Except cry, something he'd sworn he would never do again. But this was sneaky. He clenched his jaw and fought the prickliness around his eyes. The lump in his chest had a life of its own.

Earl saw his distress and rolled to his feet. He got

two cold cans of coke, handed one to Bazza and flopped back into his bean bag. He popped his can and probed gently. 'Wanna talk about it?'

Bazza drank. He was thirsty from his long walk. He wiped his lips with the back of his hand. Control returned, but he needed to watch it. Not long ago, even something as simple as a drink when he was thirsty, couldn't be taken for granted. 'What about?'

'Life in the city. How you got by. Can't have been easy?'

Bazza hesitated. Words trickled out. 'Lots of kids on the street. We made out.'

'How? What did you do for tucker?'

'Grabbed fruit, or whatever, and ran.'

'Shop keepers'd soon catch onto that wouldn't they? Watch out for you?'

Bazza nodded. 'Kept movin'. Copped a few thick ears and kicks in the behind.'

'Then what?'

'Shop liftin'. Some guys and girls got organised. One'd distract and the other'd grab. If you scored something you could sell, the money'd last a while. Save you makin' so many grab and runs.'

'That what you were doin' before you headed up here?'

'Not really. Coppers and shop owners were gettin' close. Breathin' down our necks. Those that kept at it were gettin' caught. I switched to house breakin'.'

'Bigger and bigger.'

'Yeah. Can only do that for a while then you gotta

lay low for a spell. Till things cool down.'

'What did you do in the meantime?'

'Went hungry. Or bludged off a mate.'

'How did they manage?'

Bazza stared at the floor for long moments, then drank the remainder of his coke. 'Some of the guys'd go with queers.'

Both were silent for a while, then Earl ventured the question. 'You have to?'

Bazza shook his head. 'Couldn't come at it.'

'Many of your mates help?'

'A few. No one had much. The last few months of winter were bloody tough. Had a spell when it rained and blew for over a week. One kid died. Pneumonia? Froze to death?' Bazza shrugged. 'Who knows? A warm bed and a feed looked mighty good around then.'

'That what made you head north?'

'That and the hope it would be warmer.'

Earl let out a breath of air he didn't realise he'd held. 'Phwee … and I thought I'd had it tough. When did you leave the city?'

'Dunno. End of July I think. Broke into a house in one of the northern suburbs and just kept goin'. Hit some hungry stretches. Finally landed here.' He looked across at Earl. 'Now you know. Want me to move on?'

Earl didn't hesitate. 'No! Forget what you did, it's what you do from now on that counts.'

Bazza looked at him for a moment, then turned his

head and scrubbed at his eyes. 'Must've got sand in me eyes.'

'Not surprised. Anythin' on the the beach now is gettin' sandblasted.' Earl again rolled out of his bean bag and got to his feet. 'Gunna put the kettle on and make us a brew. Whaddaya reckon?' He busied himself with the kettle.

Bazza couldn't trust his voice. He smoothed his hair back hard with both hands and looked at the floor as he fought to control his emotions. His glance settled on the magazine by Earl's bean bag. Similar ones were stacked in various places. He cleared his throat and indicated the magazine. His voice sounded tight. 'What ya readin'.'

'Fisheries newsletter.'

'What's that about?' Bazza's voice improved as he dragged his emotions into line.

'Latest on the fishin' scene. Pays to keep up with what's goin' on.'

Bazza pointed with his foot at two or three type-written pages. There was a picture of what looked like seaweed on the top one. He stabilised further as he steered the conversation away from himself. 'This from the same crowd?'

Earl looked to see what he meant. 'Naaagh. Some notes about a critter I sent to the Waterman's Bay Research Centre. Came up in a pot. Didn't know what it was.'

'What was it?'

'Sargassum fish. Funny lookin' thing. Not very big

but its side fins were almost like hands. They reckon they use 'em to hang onto the seaweed and float around with it. When a smaller fish comes near they dart out and grab it. If you look hard at the picture you'll see it. It's well camouflaged. Looks like seaweed.'

'You often do that? Send stuff?'

'Not often. Only when I come across something weird.'

'They think you're a nuisance?'

'No. Not at all. They're very helpful. I've been there a coupla times. Got to know a few of the blokes.'

'Uh-huh.' Bazza nodded. This was a whole new world. He was learning things without even thinking about it. He picked up the newsletter and flicked through it. 'Got anythin' easier?'

Earl placed the mugs on the floor between the two bean bags. 'Comic?'

'Yeah … but, maybe something a bit more … you know.'

Earl was thoughtful as he settled into his bean bag. Then he ruefully shook his head. 'Sorry. Don't think I have.'

Bazza's glance was directed at his feet. 'Yeah well. Didn't think you would. Doesn't matter anyhow.'

Silence reigned as they both sipped at their milo. Bazza's attention appeared to be centred on the contents of his mug as he posed his next question. 'Could you get somethin' down on the truck?'

'Yeah … but … Think it might be a bit public if I asked for somethin' like that over the two-way?' The decision was in Bazza's lap.

He was silent for a moment. Then he made an offhand gesture. 'Never mind. Don't really matter.'

Earl sipped at his drink then suddenly sounded business-like. 'Can do better than that. Gotta go to Geraldton in a day or two. We'll look around. Maybe ask at the library for something. Seem to remember some talk about help for people with readin' problems. One on one situation. They'll know what it's about. No one'll rubbish you.'

'Sounds interestin'.' Bazza wriggled deeper into his bean bag as another squall shrieked in additional cracks. Hadn't turned out too bad a day after all.

Two days later Bazza woke to the vibes of what was to be a bad day. Nothing he could put his finger on. On the contrary, it was a usual get-up-in-the-middle-of-the-night morning. The feeling grew as the day progressed.

Ah, to hell with it. He got on with the work. A shock at first, he now liked it. He could do it. Even felt good at his job, until he saw another boat setting pots.

The boat was from Dongara. Its skipper working an area close to where Earl had set his pots. Bazza watched the other decky as the boat ploughed along at close to full throttle. He tossed off each pot as though it was an empty carton. The rope followed high and wide, its coils free and easy before it hit the water. The floats came last, so separate and wide flung there was absolutely no chance of a snarl-up.

Bazza realised Earl was still travelling slowly to give him time to learn. He appreciated that, but now knew it made their working day longer and harder. Time he pulled his finger out.

When the first load was on board, Bazza asked Earl to step up the setting speed.

Earl looked at him. 'Reckon you can handle it?'

'Think so. Been at it a while now.'

Earl nodded. 'Okay. I'll open the throttle a bit. Watch yourself and yell if anythin' goes wrong. I'll keep an eye on you as much as I can.'

Bazza gave a thumbs up. Earl had other things to do, like watch the echo sounder to start with. He knew a lot about the sea bottom in the area but the sounder was his real eyes. Be a waste of time setting pots on flat weedy bottom. Or all sand either. Crays lived in reefs. Pots set close to a reef or on rocky bottom, caught the best.

Bazza smiled to himself. He was learning. Funny how it didn't seem like learning.

Earl cut the throttle when over the patch he wanted. He circled a couple of times and watched the black line etch across the sounder's graph paper. It looked right. He turned to Bazza. 'Patch isn't very wide, maybe six or seven pots if we set 'em close. I'll run across it. Toss 'em off as quick as you can and I'll tell you when to stop.'

'Right. That all it'll take?'

'It's long and narrow. Don't want to run the pots the other way. Be awkward pullin' 'em if the wind's from the south.'

'Got ya. We'll run two or three short lines.'

Earl grinned. 'Be skipperin' next.' He yanked open the throttle and churned *Arium* around in a tight semicircle. Bazza picked up the first pot and balanced it on the rail.

Earl eased back on the throttle and stared at the sounder. It showed eight fathoms. Then the black scratchy line crawled up the paper. 'Now!'

Bazza shot the pot into the water. He stooped, picked up the coil, turned it over and dropped it over the side. The attached floats followed high and wide. Done in perfect order, the rope was uncoiling and disappearing as it should. No danger of a twist or foul-up to 'drown' the pot.

There was no time to study his handiwork. He grabbed the next pot. It followed the first. He worked fast. Six pots went over like paratroopers jumping from a plane. He maintained the pace. Then fumbled a coil. He was looking where he was going to throw it before he picked it up. Loose coils flopped over the floats. He tried to clear them but the pull from the sinking pot snarled them tight. The tangle dragged towards the side. He yelled.

They were still over the patch but close to the edge. Earl swung round. He saw Bazza struggling with the tangle. 'Hang on!' Earl slammed the throttle shut, slapped the gear into reverse and again yanked open the throttle. The engine bellowed. Chewed water swept forward beneath the hull.

Bazza tried to hold against the drag of the pot. The tangle was hard to grip. It pulled him to the side and jammed his hands against the rail. Impact tore the rope from his fingers. The mess of rope and floats flipped over the side.

The boat bucked, still moving forward. The prop won. *Arium* stopped. Earl and Bazza stared at the tangle several metres astern. Then the boat butted its square stern back towards it.

Earl grabbed the gaff and slapped it in Bazza's hand. 'Down to the stern! You might get it before it goes!'

Bazza scrambled over the stacked pots. He reached the stern and knelt in the bait tray. The boat closed the gap. He stretched out. Another metre. The tangle tightened, slid beneath the surface.

Earl watched the floats get yanked under. 'Bastard!'

Bazza felt hollow.

Earl stared at the deck for a moment. Then looked at Bazza. 'When something like that happens, brace your foot against the gunwale and lean back. Sometimes works. Give me time to stop the boat.'

'Sorry.'

'Not to worry. We all gotta learn. Drowned a few myself over the years.'

'Might untangle underwater. Enough to let somethin' surface?'

'Doubt it. Looked like a right snarl-up.'

Bazza felt the acid of guilt. 'Better dock me pay …' Make a mess of his week's cheque. A pot, rope and floats cost plenty and he sure stuffed up dropping that one.

Earl shook his head. That wasn't an option. He put the engine in neutral and studied the area. Nothing surfaced but he spotted a white float like a light green patch deep in the water. 'Drowned it all right.'

'Isn't there anything we can do?'

Earl thought for a moment. 'One chance.' He ducked into the wheelhouse and emerged with goggles and snorkel.

Surprised, Bazza glanced shoreward. The new sun made it too hazy to distinguish landmarks. A lot of water lay between the beach and them. 'What're you gunna do?'

'Go over the side.'

'Out here?' Short line fishing spells flashed into his mind. Sometimes they hooked decent sized sharks. Some they landed, some they didn't. They all had a mouthful of sharp teeth and a body full of spring-steel energy.

'It's only water. Don't think of what might be in it.'

Bazza shut his mouth. He couldn't do it. As Earl stripped off his shirt, Bazza asked another question. 'Can you dive that deep?'

'Doubt it. But I'll be able to see better and guide the grapnel to it.'

'What can I do?'

'Take the boat.'

'What?'

'It'll drift. You've seen me handle it. Keep it near me and watch my back.'

'Jesus! Think I can?'

'Wouldn't ask if I didn't. Just go easy on the throttle. Feel your way. Don't charge over the top of me.'

'Sure this is the best way?'

'Let's do it. Time's runnin' out.'

Earl eased the boat back. He judged the position from the direction in which the pots had so far been dropped. He put the gear in neutral as he spotted the drowned one. The surface already carried small ripples. It would be difficult to see into the water once the breeze increased.

'Right. She's yours.' Earl stuffed the snorkel mouthpiece into his mouth and dropped over the side. When he surfaced he let out a yell. It expressed his shock at the water's coldness. He held up his hand.

Bazza handed him the rope and grapnel, then stood by the wheel. He watched as Earl kicked forward and let the grapnel slide down.

The boat's bow drifted to the left. Bazza engaged forward and opened the throttle. *Arium* straightened up into the light breeze. It was now some metres downwind of Earl and drifting further away.

Earl swam backwards and forwards. Bazza guessed he was trying to hook the drowned rope and floats. The gap between them widened.

Bazza swung the boat in an arc. It was more complicated than he realised. He circled around to get back into line. The problem was to not run over one of the already dropped pots. He would be even more unpopular if he ran over and chopped up another set of floats.

Upwind of Earl, he stopped the boat with a short burst of reverse. Bazza was surprised at the buzz it gave him. A big first! He was in control of a boat! The negative feelings brought on by his drowning of the pot dissipated slightly.

The boat drifted closer, threatened to drift onto Earl. Bazza gave it a burst ahead. Once it had drifted past he kicked it around in a semicircle to again position it upwind. As he stopped he felt the wind on the side of his face. It was picking up.

Earl lifted his face from the water, gave a thumbs up. Bazza let the boat drift.

When *Arium* loomed over him, Earl held up the rope. 'Keep it taut. Wrap it around the rail and hold on!'

Bazza did as he was told. Earl swarmed over the side and joined him. Between them they hauled on the rope, carefully at first so as not to dislodge the grapnel's tenuous grip. The tangle appeared. They grabbed it and heaved it over the side. Earl grunted with satisfaction as his hand closed on the rope below the tangle. 'Got it!' He heaved. When the pot broke the surface, Bazza leaned over and grabbed the bridle. They hauled the pot over the side.

Bazza felt a wave of relief. They were out of the mess. At the same time, he realised such a retrieval would have been impossible if the wind was stronger. He made a silent vow to master this pot-tossing-over business if it was the last thing he did. Others could do it. So would he.

The rope untangled and recoiled, Earl reorientated himself and cruised back to the patch. He looked at his decky. Bazza was ready with a pot poised on the rail.

'Okay. Here we go again. I'll take it slower.'

'Not too much slower. I've gotta learn. And don't worry. I won't make the same mistake again.'

Earl smiled at the positive tone in his decky's voice. Good for him. He positioned the boat. Yelled: 'Right!' as the graph etched upwards. He kept the boat marginally slower but divided his attention equally between Bazza and the sounder. Bazza concentrated and the run went smoothly. Earl gave him a thumbs up. Bazza gave a quick grin, grabbed another pot. He swung it onto the rail. He was ready.

Earl swung the boat around and they did one more run across the patch. Again it went smoothly. Bazza felt good as he looked back at the three short lines. He'd got them over well. It wasn't brute force, it was timing and concentration. Next time he'd do it even faster.

Three days later Bazza was firing on all six. He had the game by the throat. He got faster by the day and no more pots were drowned. He even found time to size some of the crays. Earl didn't have to stop so often so they could both get stuck into it.

The undersized ones, the 'cackers', were tossed over the side as quickly as possible. As Earl explained, the less damage and trauma they suffered, the sooner they would grow and become size. And the closer they were to their home ground, the sooner they would be in shelter and hidden from predators.

Some of the sea's many mysteries occasionally came up in a pot. When one did end up on the deck, or in the cacker box, Bazza flicked it aside so he could examine it later. Earl was always ready to explain. When stumped, he looked it up in one of his books back at the shack. As a last resort he sent it to the Woodman's Point Research Station. Not many fishermen bothered but Earl was interested in the environment in which he worked.

Bazza caught the bug. But most of all, he wanted to do his job well. He'd got away from the street, and was determined to give it his best shot. Might not get a second chance. His pot stacking improved. No matter how the deck pitched or rolled, he kept his feet, balanced the awkward weights and no longer staggered about like a back alley wino. Even the pots no longer felt as heavy.

The other bug to grab him was the lure of the next pot. When they hit a good patch, and each pot came up with more and more crays, anticipation egged him on. He could hardly wait to see the next pot crash over on the tipper. Such times made up for the drudgery when the catch was lean.

When a good line was loaded, he was impatient to reset it and move on to the next. His stepped up pot handling convinced him he was nearly as expert as the other deckies he spotted. It gave him a lot of satisfaction. He was close to the first goal he had ever set himself.

Then, halfway through a line, a call came on the two-way. Earl shut off the throttle, turned up the volume. He normally paid little attention to the chatter. Bazza was usually too far away to hear it over the blare from the exhaust. This call was the one every fisherman hopes he will never need to make. The one which grabbed immediate attention.

'Mayday! Mayday!'

The screamed plea was from Bert Malleton, skipper of the *Mercury*. He gave his position as ten nautical miles north-west of Port Denison. His crewman, Tim Bartle, had gone overboard with a rope tangled around his arm!

Earl calculated. *Mercury* was twenty nautical miles north of *Arium*. At full speed it would take two hours to get there. Bert needed to get his decky up quickly or it would be too late.

Several other skippers chipped in, their messages terse. They were on their way. The closest, *Centurion*, was at least ten minutes away. Earl and Bazza looked at one another. Bazza had a mental flashback to their drowned pot. What if the rope had been around his wrist? Or foot? A cold knot formed in his stomach.

The skipper of the *Mercury* didn't answer. Earl and Bazza visualised what was taking place. They stood motionless and listened to the exchanges between the boats charging to his assistance. All radio chatter ceased.

Bert Malleton heard the calls but did not reply. The skippers knew why. He had charged his boat around and headed back to where they had dropped the last pot. The floats had not surfaced. Tell tale smears of oil from the bait were already dispersing.

He stopped where he estimated his entangled decky must be. He leaned over and peered into the water. Nothing! He grabbed the grapnel. Dropped it over the side. The rope straightened. It was too short.

Nerves jumping, he whipped up the grapnel. Dropped it on the deck and scrambled to the bait tray at the stern. He scooped up a spare pot rope. Skin sheared off his shin as he scrambled over the stacked pots to get back to the wheel. It went unnoticed. He untied the grapnel rope from the rail and joined it to the longer coil. His fingers flew. Seconds felt like minutes. Minutes like hours.

In panic-induced fury he again dropped the grapnel over the side and payed out the rope. He stared into the water. The smear of oil had drifted downwind. So had the boat. The light wind was enough.

He looked up. Floats bobbed, marking previously dropped pots. He judged where the drowned one should be. He let the grapnel dangle, nudged the boat forward and around so he would be slightly upwind of the estimated spot.

Sick with dread, Bert ran up and down the deck,

dragging the grapnel back and forth in an effort to cover as much area as possible. The grapnel stayed free.

A frantic glance at the downwind set of floats told him they were too close. He'd drifted over the drowned one. He let the grapnel dangle, slapped the gear into forward and yanked back on the throttle. The exhaust bellowed. *Mercury* charged around in a tight semicircle. He churned the propeller in reverse. The boat stopped. He panted. Almost cried with frustation.

He seized the grapnel and dragged it back and forth. The boat again drifted down on the drowned pot. His mind baulked at applying the term to his entangled crewman. He gasped for breath. Flung quick glances at the next set of floats. Had he drifted too far? Should he hang on a bit longer?

He made two more passes along the side of the boat. He was about to jump back to the wheel when a movement off to the side flicked at his eye. He jerked up his head. A boat closed fast. It was less than half a mile away. White spray jetted from beneath its bow. He spotted others. All converging on him.

Relief and dismay hit him together. Help was close! But it meant at least ten minutes had rocketted by. Then the grapnel snagged.

His attention snapped back to the rope. He hauled carefully. When the grapnel held, he layed into the rope with a madman's frenzy. His muscles screamed at the combined weight of pot and decky. He fought on. Panic-pumped adrenalin surged through him.

He was afraid to breathe as he arm over armed the rope. The grapnel swept into view. Only one hook was snagged. Its tenuous hold was immediately below the second float. He leaned over, reached for the main rope. His hand viced onto it. He exhaled an explosion of held in breath and sucked in badly needed oxygen.

He straightened, dragged the rope towards the winch. Struggled it into the groove of the winch head. Stretched for the controls and yanked open the throttle. The winch picked up speed. Rope snaked onto the deck faster than he could pull it by hand.

With one hand on the throttle, he leaned over the side and stared into the water. Tim Bartle loomed up. His entangled arm broke the surface. Bert slammed the throttle closed and whipped the rope from the winch. He held it tight, swung to the side and made it fast to the rail. There was no way he'd let it slip. The pot dangled a few metres below.

He leaned down. Grasped Tim's shoulders. Heaved him half out of the water. His bent-over back screamed at the weight. He could lift no further. Tears of exhaustion and frustation welled in his eyes. He froze. He was wracked with pain, fear, guilt, dread and a total feeling of helplessness.

The bump went unnoticed. *Centurion* stopped on the opposite side. Another thud as the boat's decky leapt on board. He jumped to Bert's assistance. Reached down and gripped Tim. A powerful surge and the entangled decky was heaved over the side. He flopped onto the deck. Mark Emmerson, the newly arrived decky, grabbed the rope leading to the pot and heaved it aboard to release the pressure on the tangle.

Brian Schofield secured *Centurion* alongside and leapt on board. He ignored the tangle and rolled Tim onto his back. He began mouth to mouth. He knew the basics but had never put it into practice. It was a hell of a time to learn. Bert collapsed on the deck, drained by shock and strain.

Brian glanced at him. He appreciated the state he was in, but knew he must be kept going. Shock could damage. He paused and barked orders. 'Get on the blower! Tell 'em you're on your way. Get an ambulance on the jetty. Quick! Jump to it!'

The sharpness of the tone smashed through Bert's shock-befuddled mind. He scrambled to his feet, shot into the wheelhouse and grabbed the mike.

Brian spoke quietly to his own decky. 'Mark. Get back on board. Cast off and follow us.'

Mark moved across the deck, jumped back onto *Centurion*. He untied the ropes.

Even before Bert finished his call, Brian bellowed at him to head for home. Fast!

Earl and Bazza had not moved since the drama began. They heard the talk between the boats as they ploughed to the scene. Now they heard Bert's report.

Bazza looked at his skipper. 'Be okay, do you reckon?'

Earl hesitated. 'Don't like his chances. Between ten and fifteen minutes. At that depth ...'

'Ambulance will be ready won't it?'

Earl's brief nod gave no reassurance. 'Take *Mercury* an hour to reach Denison ...'

Bazza looked at his feet. 'Jesus.'

The silence dragged. Earl swung back to the controls. His voice was gruff. 'Come on. Let's pull these pots. Not a damned thing we can do about it.' He paused with his hand on the gear lever. He looked at his decky and his voice lost its gruffness. 'Don't think we need to break any records do you, Bazz?'

Bazza shook his head. He recalled Earl's earlier comment. The sea doesn't give you many chances. The lesson was carved into Bazza's mind. He'd had one chance.

The funeral was held mid-afternoon so as many fishermen as possible could attend. The small church was packed. Many stood outside the door. Those who finished early were cleaned up. Some were barefooted and still in their salt-stained clothes. The feeling was sombre. What had happened to Tim could happen to any of them.

A long procession of cars, utes and four-wheel drives followed the hearse to the cemetery. Family and relatives were far outnumbered by those connected to the fishing industry. All listened to the ceremony at the grave side with bowed heads. After the coffin was lowered and condolences were offered to the family, the gathering drifted into small groups.

Bazza felt like a spare part. It was the first funeral he'd been to. Kids who died on the street just disappeared from the scene. He guessed they were buried somewhere, by someone. Nothing as clean and … he groped for the word … meaningful? He took his cues from Earl and tagged along. Close enough to feel 'connected', but not close enough to get involved. There were a few nodding acquaintances among the deckies. Other than that, he knew no one.

He expected to be ignored, and was surprised when complete strangers said good day to him. Probably figured where he fitted into the scene when they saw him with Earl. The aroused feelings baffled him, until he realised, in a tentative way, he did belong. He was part of a loose organisation of people who stuck together when the going got tough. They might chiak one another over some imagined encroachment on another's 'territory', but if someone was in trouble, they rushed to help. In this instance, Earl had been too far away. If he'd been closer, they'd have been right in it.

Belonged? Bazza tried to work out what it really meant. As he followed Earl, although he couldn't quite nail it, he decided it was a good feeling.

Earl spotted Bert Malleton with a group of his close friends and moved towards him. Bazza guessed who he was. Pain and anguish were etched on the older man's face. It brought home to him what a harrowing experience it still was for the skipper. Tim was shot of his worries. Bert would carry his memories for a long time.

Bazza watched as Earl threaded his way through the group. Bert lifted his downcast face. They gripped hands but neither man said anything. Bazza realised it wasn't necessary. What had happened was a risk of the job. Acceptance was part of it. The handshake demonstrated their togetherness. The attachment that he felt warmed Bazza, even if he was only on the fringes. He was no longer a piece of flotsam.

The crowd drifted from the cemetery. Earl and Bazza drove slowly down the main street. As if drawn by a magnet, Earl pulled into the crowded parking area in front of the Dongara hotel. He looked at his crewman. 'Just a couple?'

Bazza nodded. He knew how his skipper felt about 'pissing it against the wall.' He earned his money the hard way. He couldn't see the point in giving large chunks of it to the publican. He had better things to do with it.

Bazza was no stranger to the stuff that mushed your brains. Booze, drugs, glue, it all sent you loopy. Some faster than others. Hooked kids destroyed themselves. Became pathetic bundles of rags in a stinking room in a half demolished building. Some hung on like walking zombies. He'd tried some, but once bitten, twice shy. It was a trap. Get hooked and you stole to feed the habit. The more money you needed, the worse things you did. It was a hell train to nowhere.

They talked with their contemporaries for half an hour. And felt the better for it.

Back in the ute, Earl sat and stared at nothing in

particular. He finally spoke. 'Okay. I'm not the best skipper around here. Some guys catch a lot more than I do. Take more risks too. But ...' He suddenly looked at Bazza and a wry grin chased the thoughtfulness from his face. 'Who the hell wants to bust a gut to hand over a small fortune to the tax man?'

Bazza nodded in reply. The question didn't need an answer.

Life returned to routine. Nothing untowards happened until a morning a week later. Earl woke to an empty shack. Bazza wasn't there. So? He had a day off. Days off, as distinct from days when the weather stopped him, were few and far between. He should be pleased. He wasn't. It was an enforced day off.

It was going to be a beasterly easterly. A chop maker. A slop thrower. Even so, he wanted to go out. He and Bazza had placed a small load of pots on some interesting looking bottom. Only a slight lift in the sea floor, the increased darkness of the etched sounder line indicated it could be rock, or coral. Might contain holes and crevices, home sweet home to a multitude of crays.

As far as he could recall, no one had recently worked the area. He certainly hadn't. Paid to keep an eye on what happened around you. Be a mistake to put pots on an area just extensively fished by someone else.

Earl liked the look of the patch. Unfortunately, there was no way of knowing if he was right until the pots were pulled on the following day. If the pots came up loaded, he'd plaster the patch with twice as many. It could last several days. If so, he'd record the landmarks for the future. Many similar references half filled a note book begun when he first started working for himself. Most were committed to memory but records were handy when it needed a jog.

To Earl, anticipation was the lure of crayfishing. You set your pots and then could hardly wait to find out if you'd hit the jackpot. It was a day to day treasure hunt. Only this time he had to wait until the second day. Some crays would get out. Or octopus would eat them. They were the worst cray stealers of the lot. One octopus could empty a pot like a guy could empty a bar with a smoking stick of dynamite in his hand.

The mongrels always grabbed the largest cray, broke it and sucked it clean. And the crays knew it. If an octopus got into a pot, the crays went crazy. They rocketted around inside until they found the entrance and flipped out. Earl got great satisfaction in slicing off the head of any octopus still in the pot when it slammed onto the tipper. Frustratingly, most of them oozed out on the way up.

Bazza had cray poisoning in his foot. A hazard of the job. Earl had had it himself at different times, in hands and feet. It was very painful, like stabbing needles, and it was dangerous. If it wasn't cleared up, it could lead to blood poisoning.

Penicillin killed the germ. Problem was, the antibiotic could be obtained only on a doctor's prescription. That meant a trip to Geraldton. Having chewed up the innards of the water pump, Earl's ute was in dry dock. Bazza had gone up on the cray truck as far as Dongara the previous afternoon. Earl organised a lift from there with a fisherman who lived in Geraldton but fished at Dongara. Bazza should be back around midday. He should be on the road to recovery by then, and with a bit of luck, would have a replacement water pump for the ute.

Earl badly wanted to pull those pots. The new ground enticed him as he hoped the bait was doing to the crays. Looked like he'd miss a good day's catching from it. He mentally shrugged and pulled the blankets around his neck. So be it, at least the patch couldn't run away. The crays would be there tomorrow, or the day after. Then another thought struck him. Unless another boat beat him to it!

That did it. Earl rolled out of bed. Between deckies, he worked the boat on his own. It was slower and harder and you couldn't set the pots as thoroughly. Not if you wanted to get through them all. Sometimes he was lucky to get through half of them.

This time, he'd concentrate on the new patch. If it was good, he'd reset the pots and add more to them. Probably only pull a third. The rest could wait.

The easterly was light to start with and he hoped he had misjudged it. Not so, the wind increased as the sun rose. Earl cursed it. He'd been caught that way before. Trouble was you were well and truly at sea by then. You stuck it out and battled on.

The trip out was deceptively easy. Earl was not taken in by it. The wind seems easier when you're travelling with it. He swung the boat head to wind and pulled the first pot. A blind man would have known it was full. The flapping tails and rustling shells sounded like a caged southerly. His yell was whipped away by the wind.

There were ten pots on the patch. By the time nine were pulled, one bag was full and the cacker box was overflowing. Crays crawled on the deck. Earl watched where he put his feet. The pots would yield well over two bags.

Before he pulled the final pot, he reset a freshly baited one as a marker. Just as well he did. The boat was blown away from the patch as he processed that last one. When he checked with the sounder, the reset one had missed by ten metres. The pot had drifted before it hit the bottom. He allowed for it when he reset the rest of the pots. Then picked up the first one and reset it so it too was on the patch.

Satisfied, he bagged the crays and headed east. The wind hit its straps. Gusts tried to shift the sea to Africa. Water trickled down his body from the slop chucked over him by the aggressive waves.

His next cluster of pots was on a coral patch a quarter of an hour's travel further in. He amended that. In this wind it would take twenty, twenty-five minutes. He cut the throttle to a little over half. Steep sided waves hit like brick walls. As the bow split them sheets of water sprayed into the air. Solid dollops followed, but at least while travelling, he could shelter behind the wheelhouse.

The first twelve pots yielded a bare quarter of a bag. Earl didn't need to be a genius to know it was time to shift them. The previous day he got half a bag. The day before, a bag. Ah well, nothing lasted forever. You just kept moving and trying.

It took a long while to pull, empty, rebait and load the pots. Working on his own, it not only took longer to process each pot, it took longer to reach it. While he attended to one pot, the wind blew *Arium* downwind. He then had to punch back to the next one. It was like taking one step forward and two back.

As he approached the second last pot, *Arium* buried her bow into a particularly nasty slop. Wind-whipped water leapt the gunwale. Splat! Earl shook water from his face. Rat tails of hair dripped salt water into his eyes.

He swiped it away and spotted the float in the slashed foam. He hacked down at it with the gaff. The hook snared the rope and he hauled in on board. The winch did the rest. There were only five crays in the pot. None were size.

He stacked the pots two high. As he winched each pot, the boat wallowed broadside on to the steep waves. It was wise to keep the load low.

He plonked the second last pot flat on the deck. His body worked hard to match the crazy rolling and twisting. He was used to it, but even so, the occasional abrupt movement caught him off balance.

Back at the wheel he slapped the engine into gear and yanked open the throttle. The engine bellowed. A rooster tail of water churned from beneath the hull. The boat settled its stern and shouldered around.

He cut diagonally across to reach the last pot. The closeness of the waves barely allowed the bow to break one crest before it corkscrewed into the next. Cold spray and endless pitching almost made Earl wish he'd stayed in bed. Almost. The thought of the crays on the new patch spurred him on. He punched on as wind-hurled wave tops slashed into the wheelhouse. Frothed water fanned across the screen. He poked his head past the side of the wheelhouse and spotted the last set of floats. Beyond them he spotted something else. A savage patch!

The easterly often pushed the slops into patches of three waves that were bigger and closer together. One such patch charged towards him. He jerked his head in, spun the wheel and gave the engine full throttle for a few seconds. Then slammed it off. The boat tucked in its tail, pointed her bows at the onrushing waves. It shouldered through the first crest. The wave passed. The stern kicked up. *Arium* buried her nose in the second wave. The hull split the spumed water, heaved most of it aside. Green water washed up the windscreen. Spilled back as the boat lifted clear.

Then that wave kicked up the stern. The bow buried itself deep in the third wave. The boat shuddered. Earl felt it fight its way up. He was confident of its ability. The chunk of chopped off wave washed up onto the roof. Most poured off the sides. Some waterfalled over the back onto the deck.

The short overhang of roof kept most of it off Earl. Some found the gap between his neck and the collar of his jacket. More icy trickles crawled around his body. He cursed and slowly re-opened the throttle. The savage patch had passed.

The boat answered the twist of the wheel and bucked towards the floats. Each wave swallowed them before they again resurfaced. Earl flicked the boat out of gear. He gripped the smooth wet handle of the gaff and leaned out from the side.

The curve of the bow shouldered a chunk of wave aside. It buried the floats in a welter of foam. Earl chopped down with the gaff. Water shot up from the plunging hull. Hit him in the face. He missed.

When he cleared his eyes, the rope was beyond reach. He glanced at the grapnel. Water sluicing along the foredeck had tangled its rope. The bow fell away before the wind. In a moment the boat was again broadside on. The gap widened.

Earl spun the wheel, engaged the prop and opened the throttle. The boat churned around in a tight curve. Again he punched the boat towards the floats. This time his approach coincided with a slight lull. Even so, the rope was almost beyond reach. He made the extra effort. He leaned further out, slashed down with the steel hook. It flashed in the sunlight, sliced into the water and caught.

Broadside on once more, the boat dropped its side into a sudden trough. The deck kicked, caught Earl off balance and shot him over the side like a spear.

He dived into a charging wave. Came up spluttering, his dignity more hurt than anything else. The water was warm after the wind on his wet body. It was also deceptively calm in the trough. That disappeared as he rose to the top of the next wave. Hissing wind lashed the surface. Liquid pebbles stung his face. Spindrift filled the air.

Earl struck out for the boat. The apron and jacket hampered him. He was unworried. The boat was only metres away. He swam strongly and evenly. He grinned inwardly at being so neatly tossed overboard. Just as well no one saw it. He'd never hear the end of it.

A flick of unease stabbed through him. The gap widened. Unease jumped to alarm. He increased his stroke. The gap stayed the same. Panic erupted and he thrashed at the water.

The boat skidded sideways. Gust-torn chunks of waves lashed after it. Earl could hardly breathe in the wind-whipped spray.

His panic quickly burnt itself out. He stopped to regain his breath and get back his breathing into rhythm. Without the apron and jacket, he could catch his boat, no sweat.

Acting on the thought he trod water. He untied and stripped off the apron. The jacket was more difficult. As he lifted it up the wind plastered it to his head and body. It stuck as though glued. His upraised arms were trapped.

Earl thrashed with his legs and gulped at the air inside the jacket. He tired quickly. Keeping his arms in the air and his head above water consumed energy. How long could he keep it up?

He forced himself to think. Get rid of the jacket, before he tied himself in knots and drowned. He took a deep breath and flopped. Wallowing just below the surface, he stripped off one sleeve. Then the other. Pulled the jacket over his head.

He surfaced and refilled his lungs. He again wallowed and stripped off his shirt. His shorts followed. Free of drag, it was easier to tread water. He reorientated himself and looked for his boat.

In a trough, he could see nothing but water. It didn't matter. He knew where his boat was — downwind. A hissing crest lifted him and he peered off through the flying water. He glimpsed solid white before he slipped into another trough. Hollowness came with the glimpse. It was a hell of a long way away.

Each second widened the gap. Earl squashed his panic and slipped into a distance-eating pace. Strength needed to be rationed. At least he was heading downwind. Bashing into the slop would have been a different story. Problem was, he was swimming away from the shore and further out to sea.

Hundreds of strokes later he paused and again trod water. Swept upward by a wave, he made the most of the moment. He stared across the wave tops. A flash of hard white caught his eye. It was as far away as ever.

Fear ate deeper into his mind. Spread ice into his stomach. It would be hours before anyone missed him. And seachers would look for his boat. When they found it, with no one on board, they would look for a head in the water. A minute thing to find with the sea blasted into a billion wave slops. Who or what would find him first?

He thrashed forward. Again panic burnt him out. He floundered. Then a small flash of black and white caught his eye. A float! He lunged. His hand struck rope. Cold fingers taloned around it. He pulled it towards him and draped rubbery arms over it. He gulped air and much needed oxygen.

Moments passed. He opened his eyes and looked at the float. Read the number branded into it with a hot iron. He was hanging onto one of his own floats. Pity it wasn't someone else's. The owner might arrive to pull it.

Each time a wave lifted him, he stared downwind. Caught an occasional flash of solid white. The boat's hard outline was an alien shape in the wilderness of spumed waves. Distance was hard to estimate, but it didn't matter. The inevitable ate in like acid. He had Buckley's chance of catching it.

He felt slightly rested, but was reluctant to leave the float. He might not find another. The water, initially warm, now sucked heat from his body. Coldness moved in and made him want to urinate. With the thought came visions. He'd caught sharks both while hand fishing and on set lines. He respected their powerful jaws and sinuous bodies.

Images exploded in his mind. He expected the slash and rip of teeth at any moment. He stared at the water. The surface was too disturbed to see far into it. If one was there, he'd never see it. Until it hit! His flesh crawled.

Staring achieved nothing. Reason returned and he settled to an uneasy awareness. If one did attack, there wasn't a damned thing he could do about it.

Death seldom occupied his thoughts. Apart from the fact that it was inevitable. Nothing lived forever. He occasionally wondered what happened afterwards. But held no firm beliefs, one way or the other. It was an ephemeral thought. A bridge to be crossed when he came to it. But now?

What was dying like? Was it quick? Or prolonged agony? He guessed that depended on how it happened. By drowning? Or being chewed and torn to pieces? He shuddered. He needed help. But to whom did he cry out? Did God exist? And if he did, would he listen? Earl wasn't exactly on good terms with him. On the odd occasion when he asked for help, he'd received a big fat nothing!

Overall, Earl didn't think much of his chances. He glanced towards the east. A savage patch charged towards him. He yanked the second float his way. His ropes had two floats a couple of metres apart. Right then he needed all the flotation he could get. He wrapped his arms around them.

The pot-anchored rope pulled taut. The first hill of water surged over him. Earl kicked with his feet and surfaced in the trough at the back of the wave. He kicked harder and rose to the crest of the next wave. He shot a glance downwind. Extra height helped. He got a quick glimpse of his boat. Something about it looked odd.

He dropped into the following trough. Again he kicked. The next big wave swept him upwards. For a fraction of a second he got a clear sight. White spray leapt into the air as a wave crashed into the transom.

The sighting warmed him. Hope pumped blood into his muscles. He struggled for a confirming sight. He didn't get it.

He hung limp in the next trough. He needed every bit of stamina he possessed. It was a win or bust moment.

A minute later Earl released the floats. He wanted to take them with him. He needed the bouyancy but had nothing with which to cut them off. His numbed fingers could never untie the water tightened rope.

He struck out. He was torn between the need for haste, and the need to conserve energy. It could be a hard wave-tossed slog.

He guessed what had happened but was afraid to believe it. Only one thing would cause his boat to change from broadside on. No, it was too tenuous. He mustn't dwell on it. It tempted fate.

He slogged on. He was tired, but kept going. He maintained the steady pace. Time ate into his one slim chance. A crazy urge to thrash faster almost overpowered him. He resisted it. How he managed to, he didn't know. Right then, there was neither time nor energy to think about it.

He glimpsed the boat more often. *It was being held by the stern!* It could only be one thing. Under these conditions, that one thing could not hold for long.

A pot rope! As the boat passed over it, the rope and floats had tangled in the underwater gear. Must have washed between the skeg and the bottom of the hull. Probably wedged against the prop or rudder. Whatever, Earl hoped they'd stay jammed. Please, just a little bit longer?

He knew the wind-hustled boat would drag the pot until it hit a rock or a low reef. Judging by the way the waves belted against the transom, it had done one or the other. He said a silent prayer for the rope. The last thing he needed was a bodgy piece of rope.

Synthetic rope was tough. Tougher than the old hemp. But still vulnerable to being cut or chafed. Visions of rope sawing backwards and forwards across the curve of a propeller blade, or a jagged edge of coral, haunted him. He strained to catch another glimpse from a wave top.

He snatched one. Froth fanned upwards from the stern. Good, it was still holding. Earl spat out a mouthful of water. It was difficult to draw clear air into his lungs. He trod water and raised his face clear of the surface. He coughed the gurgle from his throat and breathed deeper.

Cold penetrated. Body warmth retreated further towards the centre. He almost gave in, then spat and cursed as another slop belted him over the head. The anger revived him. He again struck out, before the cold smothered his will to survive.

He could barely feel his legs. Like his arms, they were recycled rubber. He concentrated and moved them more or less where he wanted them.

The hull loomed. A wave kicked up the stern. It hung in the air for a moment as the peak of water passed beneath. Earl caught a flash of red anti-fouling. He also caught a glimpse of floats jammed between the prop and the skeg. A thin orange rope, as taut as steel, stretched from them.

Fear surged through him. How much strain could it take? The sight triggered a spasm through his muscles. He kicked harder. His arms curved over more strongly. He dug deeper and dragged his hands through the water. He heard the burble of the idling engine. Fumes and water spat from the black-rimmed hole in the transom.

He clawed across the last few metres. Reached out. His fingers seized the batten at the bottom of the transom. A wave cocked the stern skyward. It dropped as the boat hobby-horsed. The hull slapped down and shot out a jet of water. It hit Earl in the face. His mouth was open from his lunging effort. Water shot into his throat. He coughed, spluttered and gagged as he fought to clear it.

The stern belted up and down. Cross-hatched smaller waves came from all directions. Earl was close to drowning but still had sense enough to push his body away. If he got washed beneath the stern, a downward plunging prop blade could slice him open as quick as look at him.

Desperation froze his fingers to the slippery batten. There was little to grip. The boat bucked as though it wanted to shake him loose. Earl sensed the next downward plunge of the hull. He shot up his hand. Numbed fingers clawed into one of the deck draining scuppers, locked on its edge.

The next upsurge nearly tore his arm from its socket. He ignored the pain and fought to maintain the grip. His fingers held. On the next down-plunge, he slid his hand to the side of the scupper. Where there was more to grip.

He ignored the beating taken by his body, timed his movements to the waves. He brought his other hand up. Gripped the other side of the oblong hole. His head was above the worst of the wash. He breathed clear air more often.

He hooked his toes on the batten. All he needed was one good heave and he could claw his way onto the bait tray. Each time he tried, a squelch of water tore his toes from the weed-slimed batten. It repeatedly left him hanging by his arms.

His muscles trembled. He desperately needed a lull to enable him to pull clear of the water. He glanced over his shoulder. His fingers convulsed until they hurt. A savage patch charged at him.

The stern reared on the first crest, plunged into the following trough and was hammered by the second wave. The wall of water plastered Earl to the transsom. The blow numbed him and drove air from his lungs.

His mind went blank, but for one command. It droned one order — hang on! Mentally, he lost contact with the rest of his body. It was simply something that hung from his hands and flailed against the hard wooden hull. Water dragged at him. The bottom edge of the transom hacked at his hips and belly. Only his hands mattered. His life hung from those locked fingers.

Somewhere in the rush and slap of water, the fume-filled rumble by his ear, a crisp sound registered. His body slewed sideways. Water dragged from a different direction. The hammering eased. Dazed and half drowned, pain jerked him back to reality. Constructive awareness returned.

The rope had snapped. The boat was broadside on to the waves. Chunks of wrenched-apart floats dotted the water. Skittered away across the wave tops.

The hammering at the stern changed to a violent sideways rolling. It put Earl in slightly calmer water. He clung and rested.

After a few moments he lifted his foot and planted his toes on the batten. It took more seconds to consciously release one hand from the scupper. He trembled his leg straight, reached up and grabbed the edge of the bait tray. The second hand followed. A heave and he slipped his other foot into the scupper. Another heave and he was draped over the edge. He twisted his body and rolled into the tray. He then crawled across the scarred wood of the gunwale, over the low stack of pots and tumbled onto the deck.

The engine pulsed life into his battered body.

Minutes later, he crawled to the wheelhouse. Pulled himself up the doorframe and dug out Bazza's waterproof jacket. His legs gave way as he put it on. He didn't know if he was shivering from cold or reaction. He slopped tea from the thermos he'd brought with him. More slopped from the mug as he shook it to his lips. The hot drink helped revive him.

He finally cracked a wry grin and slapped his hand on *Arium*'s deck. 'Glad you stuck around for a bit. Contrary should be your second name.'

A thought floated at the back of his mind. Were some thanks due elsewhere? Unfortunately, he didn't know how to go about it.

Sufferin' catfish! What a morning! He took a deep breath and gave himself a mental shake. One thought loomed large. Any lingering doubts about taking Bazza on were blown to shreds. He needed him with a capital N.

Earl took his time about punching back to the new patch of ground. He reset the pots he'd picked up but did everything slowly and methodically. He never overextended himself. He realised there would be some tidying up to do when the sea was calmer. Like picking up that last pot where he nearly came to grief. And when the sea was really calm, maybe pick up the pot from which the floats had been smashed. Synthetic rope was itself buoyant, and not being tangled, the top end might reach the surface. He could guess at its position from those on the new ground.

He headed in. Ironically, the closer he got to shore, the smaller the waves became. By the time he punched back to the anchorage, the water carried little more than ripples. The wind was now fitful, a sign it would peter out in the early afternoon.

Earl shook his head. That was a beasterly easterly for you. Calm at the water's edge, hell when you got out a few miles. Ah well, no good crying about it. He reached out and shut off the engine. As the boat lapsed into silence and tugged gently at its mooring chain, he gave the back of the wheelhouse a light kick.

'You mightn't be a thing of beauty you old bastard, and you stink a bit, but by hell I wouldn't be without you for quids.'

As he rowed ashore, his thoughts drifted back to Karl Ricks, his 'Dutch Uncle' from his Dongara fishing days. How did he cope in such weather? He always worked on his own. Maybe he never went out on such days. Naagh, that wasn't right. Karl never missed a day. How did he manage? Smaller boats tossed more. He'd need suction caps on his boots.

The rhythmic rowing action freed a thought and he suddenly sat up straight. Karl! You wily old bugger! You're still teaching me.

Bazza's limp was less pronounced when he walked into the shack around lunchtime. He carried a small box and a plastic carry bag and a cardboard carton was tucked beneath his other arm. A couple of clear plastic-covered parcels lay on top of the stores in the carton. There was no mistaking them for anything but a waterproof apron and jacket.

He put the boxes on the table but retained the carry bag. It was emblazoned with the name of a well-known Geraldton menswear store. He looked at his skipper. Earl was sprawled in a bean bag, his hair wet from the shower. Although he gave the appearance of being relaxed and comfortable, Bazza thought he looked more tired than usual. Hot and sweaty from his trip in the truck, he couldn't help having a dig. 'Some people get it easy.' Even as he said it, he sensed a mystery. Two bags of crays with

Earl's name and number on them were waiting to be picked up by the truckie.

'Somebody's gotta keep the home fires burnin'. We can't all go swannin' off to the big smoke whenever we feel like it.'

Bazza grinned. He favoured his sore foot and flopped into the adjacent bean bag. He stretched his legs out in front of him. Home. A rough shack, miles from anywhere, it meant more to him than any dwelling he'd ever known. So? Why feel edgy?

Earl noticed the improvement in Bazza's walk but asked anyway. 'How's the foot?'

Bazza lifted it. 'Didn't chop it off. Was tempted to do that myself a day or two ago. Think I'll keep it now. That penicillin sure acts quick. Feelin' better already. Be right by tomorrow.'

Earl nodded. 'Good. But don't stop till you've finished the course of tablets. Clean it right up. If you only half kill it, it'll take off again and you'll be worse off than before. Did you get the water pump from Coventry's?'

'Yep.'

'No problems?'

'Nope.' Bazza couldn't hide the pleasure in his voice. 'Read him your note.'

Earl caught the emphasis on the word 'read'. 'Is that a fact? Caught up with the teacher then?'

Bazza nodded. 'Mrs Castle. Squeezed me in for an extra session. We worked on lots of things, but mostly chewed on your note until I had it right.' He didn't say it but he felt ten feet tall when he read it to the guy in Coventry's.

Earl nodded his approval. 'Good on you, Bazz. What's she like?'

'Nice. Doesn't take the mickey outta ya.'

'Young or old?'

'Pretty old. Got kids in high school.'

Earl figured she was around forty. Seen from Bazza's age that probably was old. He indicated the carton on the table. 'Got the stores okay?'

'Yep.' Bazza's unease returned. 'Truckie said you'd ordered the apron and jacket on the two-way. How come?'

'Aww … chucked the others away. Reckoned it was time I had some new ones.'

Bazza was surprised by the answer. He couldn't put his finger on it but his unease sharpened. He knew from his time on the street that it didn't pay to ask questions. Nevertheless, his unease pushed him. 'Two bags of crays waiting for the truckie?'

Earl made an imaginary tick in the air. 'Give the man his badge for observation.'

Bazza still probed. 'Easterly would've been a bummer.'

Earl nodded. 'You could say that.'

'What made you go?'

'Wanted to pull those pots we put on that new patch. Came up trumps so I added some more to it. Looks like being a real bonanza.'

Bazza felt the drag of dismay. So that was it.

Shouldn't have gone to Geraldton. He was surprised at the pain he felt. The carry bag dropped from his fingers. It suddenly lost its importance. It took him a while to find his voice. When he did, it came out strangled. 'Is this the boot?'

'What?' Earl was startled.

'Marchin' orders?'

'No way! Man, I've never needed anyone more in my life!'

The sharpness of the reply caused Bazza to lift his head. He stared as his skipper. The words squeezed out like drops from a bitter lemon. 'Didn't need me this mornin'.'

'Jeez! If you only knew.'

'Then tell me.'

Earl looked back at him. He shot his pride down in flames and told Bazza exactly what happened. 'Make no mistake, Bazz, I need you.'

Bazza stared at the floor. He commented softly. 'Like you once said, the sea doesn't give you many chances.'

Earl answered as softly. 'Yeah. That's why I need you. Why we need each other. No matter what happens to one of us, the other one is there to help.'

Silence reigned. Bazza felt relief, followed by the strange emotion he'd experienced before. Being needed was something he was still unfamiliar with. It took him a while to get his act together. When he did, his voice came out gruff. 'Reckon what we both need is a good feed. You had any lunch?'

'Quick snack. Thought you'd be along around now.'

'Waitin' for me to do the cookin' I'll bet.'

Earl held up his hand and rolled out of his bean bag. Bazza noticed his movements were slower than usual. He favoured some muscles. Must've been really rough.

Earl poked around in the stores box. 'Should be some steak here. Hope Chris gave us his best. I'll chew his ear if he didn't.' He found what he was looking for. 'Right! Now I'm gunna cook you a feed that'll make you wanna shed your shell.'

Bazza grinned and wriggled deeper into his bean bag. This he could take.

Earl continued the conversation as he bustled at the stove. 'Could have another surprise for you.'

Bazza looked up. 'Good one?'

'Think so.'

'Found a way to make the easterly stop?'

'I said a surprise, not a miracle.'

'Okay. What is it?'

'Gunna sleep in tomorrow.'

Bazza's eyebrows shot up. 'That'll be a first. What brought that on?'

'Karl Ricks taught me another lesson.'

'That the old guy you said was your Dutch Uncle? He been down?'

'No. Remembered something. Something I saw him do.'

'Like what?'

'Unless I miss my guess, weather'll be the same tomorrow.'

'Think me foot's suddenly gone bad.'

Earl grinned. 'Yeah and I'm off swimmin' for a while. No, I remembered seein' Karl go out around midday a coupla times. At the time I thought the old bugger was slowin' down. The years were catchin' up with him.'

'Perhaps they were.'

'Karl slow down? Never! No, he was waitin' for the easterly to blow itself out.'

Bazza grasped the significance. He'd now been in the game long enough to know the easterly usually petered out in the afternoon. 'So you reckon ...?'

'Yeah. We'll give it a go. Take off around eleven. When the beasterly starts to gust. By the time we reach the pots it'll have blown its guts out. Few crays might get out, but what the hell?'

Bazza digested the idea. Sounded good. Definitely worth a try. He grinned up at his skipper. 'Better watch it though. Next thing we'll be wishing for easterlies.'

'Don't kid yourself, these beasterly easterlies can't last much longer. Once that high in the bight moves over to cook the South Aussies, we'll be back into the southerlies.'

Bazza shrugged. 'Ah well, you win some you lose some.'

Earl glanced at him and noticed the carry bag Bazza had shoved aside. 'What've you got there?'

Bazza grinned and pulled the bag onto his lap. He looked even younger than his years. He plunged in his hand. Out came a brand new pair of jeans. The smell of newness was noticeable when he held them up. 'What d'ya reckon?'

Earl showed interest. Reached across and felt the material. 'Very swish. They rob you?'

'Nope. They were marked down. Couldn't resist 'em.' He vividly recalled how he felt when he pulled the money out of his pocket and paid for them. Money he'd earned!

On Earl's advice, he'd booked a motel room and would be hard pressed to describe how he felt when he walked into it. It was unreal. He could legitimately occupy the unit until the following morning. He'd paid for it. It was his. He had as much right to it as anyone. He could have a shower. Use the phone. Do practically anything.

Not that there was anyone to ring. Except Mrs Castle. He rang her immediately. Felt awkward, had trouble communicating, but eventually explained what he wanted. He was buoyed by the help he received. After the initial embarrassment, it was nice to talk to her. Better than his hesitant, scratchy attempts at writing sent on the truck. Even better than her encouraging replies Earl helped him read.

Earl had given him the cash for his short stay. In case he had trouble getting money from his own account. And he did have a tidy sum in the bank.

That was another first. Earl had helped him to open the account. His weekly cheque went straight into it. When he was familiar with words and forms, he'd take care of such things himself.

Bazza refolded the jeans and slid them back into the bag. He wriggled into his bean bag. He hoped his pleasure wasn't too obvious. Inside, he felt like a kid at his own slap-up birthday party.

The stratagem worked well. They went out late for two days of screaming easterlies. Under calmer conditions, the pots were pulled more quickly and easily. Bazza tucked the information away. You sure learnt in funny ways.

The weather pattern moved. Southerlies returned. Things went well for a week. The crays were active. Catches were good. Earl hoped they'd keep it up a bit longer. He needed another week's good catching. Then the wind lightened. Earl wondered if it was the start of the calms of April/May. He hoped not. Not yet.

Then the full moon coincided with an April calm. Bazza had never seen the sea so clear. Or the nights so bright. The crays backed into their hideaways and stayed there.

After a pull yielded only a quarter of a bag, Earl decided to try for bait. Instead of being at sea, early morning found them on the beach several kilometres north of the anchorage. The ute was parked nearby. Bazza lost the toss and waded out with the net piled on a makeshift float, a piece of marine ply lashed to an inflated tube. The net fed off as he quietly waded out into water up to his chin, then moved parallel to the beach for fifty metres before coming back to shore. They began the steady pull-in.

Bazza broke the working silence. 'Crays often go this quiet?'

'Full moon *and* flat calm sea. They no likee.'

'Go crazy or somethin'?'

Earl grinned at the vision of a heap of crays dancing around like idiots. 'Naagh. Just don't crawl.'

'None of 'em?'

'Few. Hardly worth goin' out for. Unless there's a stir-up to dirty the water. Or cloud to cover the moon.'

'How long for?'

'Coupla days. Maybe a week. Depends on the weather.'

'And nothing inbetween?'

'Might get a few on a two day pull. Not worth goin' out every day. Cost too much for fuel and bait.'

'This'll help then.' Bazza leaned into the pull.

'Hope so. Could use a bit of help right now. Might try night fishin'. Coupla hundred kilos of dhuies would help.'

'Run of whites was okay, wasn't it?'

'We did all right, but not as good as I'd hoped. That's why I've got an appointment with the bank manager today.'

'What's he want?'

'What do all bank managers want? I've got a boat payment due.'

'Thought Kailis financed you?'

'Gear, yes. Guaranteed my loan at the bank for the boat. Up to me to do my bit. Unfortunately, the whites are a bit hit-and-miss. If you're in the right place at the right time, you make a killin'. If not, you go hungry. We'll make it up on the reds. Always have in the past. Just gotta convince the manager.'

'That why you made that graph thing last night.'

'Jeez! You're askin' a lot of questions this mornin'!'

'Sorry.'

Earl stopped pulling the net. He stood up straight, took a deep breath, then slowly exhaled. 'No, you're right, Bazz. Fire away. How else you gunna learn things. I'm a bit edgy this mornin'. Bank managers do that to me.' He again bent to the task. 'The graph shows my catch month by month since I started fishin'. Managers like figures, so I'll show him some.'

Bazza nodded. 'Keeping records isn't only for the Fisheries Department?'

'You got it.'

They fell silent again as they worked in the net. Bazza was enjoying, for the thousandth time, the freedom of being in the open and away from street pressures. The thought again flicked through his mind, it was damned nice not to have to watch his back. No one was gunna take advantage of him out here.

He heard a splash, looked up. Spotted some rea-

115

sonable sized fish darting around in the closing circle. He was trying to work out what they were when Earl surprised him.

'Looks like I'll be needin' a new decky.'

Bazza felt a flick of unease. 'Why? What've I done?'

Earl chuckled. 'Nothin' wrong. I'm talkin' a coupla years. Don't reckon you'll be content to be a decky forever.' He paused as he moved forward a pace to get space at his feet for more net. 'That's how it should be. Stick with your readin' and writin', no matter how hard it seems.'

Earl and Bazza walked up the beach and hauled the catch onto the hard wet sand. The sun, shining at a low angle, flashed on the trapped fish as they flapped and squirmed in the mesh of the net. Bazza enthused as they examined them.

'Cop that beauty!'

Earl nodded. 'King whiting. He and a few others'll go well in the frypan. Rest are mullet. Should do at least one day's bait-up.'

'Worth another run? Bit further up the beach?'

'Probably. But we don't have time. Gotta mooch if I'm gunna make that meetin'.'

Earl walked the few metres to get a clean bag from the ute. Something caught his eye as he turned back. He jerked up his head and stared out to sea. 'What was that?'

Bazza looked up from the catch. 'What was what?' He followed Earl's gaze. The sea was placid. The sky an unmarked blue. A good day to be pulling pots. Pity.

'Thought I saw somethin'.'

'What sort of somethin'?'

'Smoke. Thought for a moment it was the tail end of a parachute flare.'

'I didn't see anythin'.'

Earl nodded. 'Probably imagined it. Come on, let's get these stowed. We better make tracks.' He lay the bag on the wet sand and scooped fish into it. The few large ones he tossed to one side. Bazza extracted those fish with their gills caught in the mesh of the net. He also plucked out pieces of weed.

Earl cast several quick glances seaward. 'Keep a watch though. Just in case ...'

Karl Ricks was out. He intended to pull half his gear and then do some line fishing. Deep down he was a line fisherman. He preferred it. The fact that cray-fishermen earned more money finally dragged him kicking and screaming into crayfishing. He was younger then. Thought he needed more money.

He held a sixty pot licence. Maintained he didn't catch enough to warrant a decky. In truth, his needs were small and he preferred to work on his own. Working fewer pots, he placed them more thoroughly. And he didn't waste time bending his elbow. He was a fisherman, so he went fishing. He didn't grab at every chance to have a day off. These days, youngsters had no staying power.

He pulled a pot. His gnarled old hands looked like bird talons but he could still coil a rope with the best of 'em. His winch was belt driven from the front of the engine. He had no time for these hydraulic ones. Newfangled things were full of gadgets that went wrong. He understood his old one. If a belt broke, he replaced it. If a gear stripped, he replaced it. When it came to all those valves and pipes and things, you needed to be an Einstein to know which way was up. Or you had to call in some so-called 'expert' who used a fork when he wrote out his bill.

Karl didn't have far to move when he processed a pot. Space was limited on his *Jezebel*. He liked that. A small boat meant small fuel bills. He landed the pot and tipped out its contents. There were four crays. He ran his eye over them. One *might* be size. Time to move. But to where? He should've moved them the day before. Uncharacteristically, he'd ducked the issue. Damned old bones and muscles grizzled a bit these days. He thought a moment and accused himself of going soft. Right! Meant stacking, but so be it.

He plonked the pot on the deck near the stern but stayed bent over for a few moments with his hands resting on the pot. Head felt strange. He paused for a moment longer. Then straightened, walked back to the tipper and swung the heavy iron cradle back into position.

Again he paused. Shook his head. His vision blurred. Aaargh, must be getting old. He shrugged, picked up the stainless steel cray gauge, and slowly toppled forward.

As they loaded the net into the back of the ute, Bazza saw his skipper looking to the north-west. Bazza also checked. There was nothing there. Earl must've imagined it.

Bazza glanced at the next curve of sand. He'd been well bitten by the bug. Next pull might come up with twice as many fish. 'Next bay looks interestin'. Tried it?'

'Not for a while. Have to wait for another day. Time we headed back. Bank managers, like tides, wait for no man. Especially when that man owes 'em money.'

'Pity.'

'In more ways than one. Never mind, Bazz, we'll be back.' Earl paused as he was about to get into the ute. He again scanned the horizon.

Bazza noticed. 'See anythin'?'

Earl shook his head. 'Thought I did earlier. Looked like a thin line of smoke just before it gets blown away.'

'There's no wind. It's flat calm.'

'Could be some further out.'

Bazza nodded. He'd seen that trick before. Could be calm when you left, but when you reached the pots, the wind pounced on you like a cat on a mouse. 'Must've been mistaken.'

'Yeah. Guess so. Still, wish I had a two-way here.'

'Wouldn't take long to shoot out to the boat.'

Earl looked at his watch. He normally didn't wear one but this day, time was important. How long would it take to get cleaned up and travel to Geraldton? Hmm. Have to be a quick splash in the shower. 'Might have time ... Yeah, damn it! Some poor bastard might be in trouble out there.' He swung into the cab. 'Come on!'

Earl raced along the hard sand to the anchorage. He skidded the ute to a stop. They threw the dinghy into the water and Bazza laid into the oars.

Once alongside, Earl flew over the side. He sprang into the wheelhouse and switched on the two-way. As soon as it was warm, he pressed the transmit button.

'6DI. This is *Arium* calling. Do you read me?'

The answer came immediately. Staff couldn't have been busy in the factory office.

'*Arium*. DI. Over.'

'Any reports of a boat in trouble? Between here and Dongara? One of the guys from up there? No one's out down here.'

'Nope. And I've been here all morning.'

'No flare sightings?'

'No. What's up?'

'Thought I caught the tail end of a parachute flare.'

'Don't think many, if any, boats have gone out from here. Been no traffic on the air. Hang on, I'll give OTC a ring. They might have received a distress call on another frequency. I'll call you back.'

'Roger.'

Earl retained the mike and looked at his watch. Better be quick. Not many minutes had passed but he was already beginning to fidget. 'Come on, Ted.'

'Appointment that important?' Bazza understood Earl's agitation. If it was them out there, broken down or sinking, he'd be hoping like hell someone would see any flare they put up. Radios did break down. All it needed was a bit of water in the wrong place.

'Yeah. This boat means a lot to me. It's not just a way of makin' a dollar, it enables me to be someone.'

'Fishermen aren't considered much in this world.'

'That's not what I meant. To hell with what anybody else thinks, I'm somebody to me! Nobody gives me any hand-outs and I'm not askin' for any. Sure I've had help but it's not charity. I'll pay back every cent if it's the last thing I do!'

Bazza was taken aback by the outburst, but he understood the emotion behind it. Six months ago he wouldn't have had a clue as to what Earl was talking about. Now he did. It just surprised him to hear Earl being so emphatic about it.

Earl saw the look on his face and grinned. 'Listen to me!' He looked around his feet. 'Where's me soapbox?'

The radio came to life before Bazza could answer.

'*Arium*. DI. Over.'

Earl thumbed the mike. '*Arium* back.'

'OTC haven't heard anything.'

'Hmm … thanks, Ted. Must've been mistaken.'

'I could get someone to check the anchorage here and see who's gone out. Be a while before I can get back to you.'

'Won't be able to hang around that long. See ya. Out. Oh, hang on! Heard of any short time skippering jobs? Could use a bit of work to tide me over this lean spell. Help get the bank manager off my back.'

'Heard the boss talking about something. I'll look into it for you.'

'Thanks, Ted. See you.'

Earl replaced the mike and switched off the two-way. He still looked thoughful.

Bazza watched him. 'What d'ya think?'

Earl looked at his watch.

'Think I've already wasted too much time.' He headed for the deck.

10

Bazza slid over into the dinghy and set up the oars. Earl started to follow, but paused with his rump on the gunwale. He gazed down at the dinghy, obviously not seeing it. Seconds ticked by. When he spoke, the words came slowly. Each one refused to be ignored. 'If that *was* a flare, then someone's in trouble ...'

'Nobody's heard or seen anything.'

'That's the problem. If someone is in trouble, his only chance of help has to come from me. And damn it! I just don't know!'

Silence again. Earl looked at his watch, then out to sea. Then back at his watch. 'Bugger it! Probably imagined it. And I can't afford to miss that appointment. Bank managers consider fishermen a bad risk at the best of times. If I don't show, he'll think I'm like his image of all fishermen, irresponsible and interested only in a bellyful of beer.' Still he hesitated. Then, he suddenly swung down and slumped in the stern of the dinghy. Bazza dug in the oars and rowed.

Earl sat with his forearms on his thighs. His hands dangled between his knees. He stared at the bottom of the dinghy but saw only one picture in his mind. A tiny wisp of smoke, if that's what it was, marking the otherwise clear blue of the sky. It disappeared from the picture but not from his thoughts.

It could have been water vapour and air expelled by a whale. He was on the beach. A blow could have been silhouetted against the horizon. The whale would have to be close in. But that was possible. Thoughts flicked on. He had scanned the sea thoroughly. Seen no sign of whale activity. Imagination? He mentally shrugged. He'd been in tight spots himself. Vividly remembered the last one. Could he ever forget? It wasn't a barrel of laughs when you were in trouble at sea.

He suddenly grabbed the oars. Dug one in and pushed deep and hard with the other. The dinghy spun round.

Bazza was surprised by the action. 'What're you doin'?'

'Can't ignore it.'

Arium was underway in minutes. Once through the inshore reef, Earl opened the throttle. White spray bird-winged from beneath the bow. The exhaust bellowed into the swirled wake. Bazza climbed onto the wheelhouse roof and scanned the sea.

Earl headed towards the area where he thought he'd seen the smoke. Waves were visible to the north-west, where the slight swell lazily humped and crashed onto the barely submerged Big Horseshoe.

He neared the inside of the reef. Craypot floats dotted the surface but there was nothing else. Bazza came down from the roof and joined Earl as he cut back on the throttle. 'Not a sausage.'

'Yeah. Blown it. The manager'll sharpen his axe.'

'Not your fault. You had to do somethin' once you sighted the flare.'

'*Thought* I sighted a flare. He'll probably put that excuse in the 'now-I've-heard-'em-all' basket.'

Bazza shrugged. 'Still might be someone out here … somewhere. Sea's a big place.'

Earl looked thoughtful. Then slowly nodded. 'Let's think this thing through.'

'Boat might've sunk.'

Earl was reminded of his own small head in the vastness of the sea. 'Hmm, could explain why we didn't see anymore flares.'

'Or why there was no radio call.'

Earl looked dubious. 'It'd have to be quick.' He indicated the sea. It was calm but for the lazy swell. 'Not very likely in this.'

'Maybe it's further out. Hard to gauge distance over water. Or it is for me.'

'You're no orphan there. Yeah, you could have a point. Could've been outside.' Earl looked at the row of curling breakers. 'Let's have a look around the back.'

Bazza climbed back onto the roof to extend his scanning range. Earl yanked open the throttle.

It took a while to reach the northern end of the reef. Earl cut it short because of the calmness of the sea. They were past where it was actually breaking. Aggressive rogues were unlikely in the existing conditions. Even so, green water humped as he turned seaward. He wasn't worried. The swells weren't too big. There would be enough water beneath the keel. Anyway, he'd be across before you could say knife.

The boat crested a green hump. Bazza glimpsed black. 'Somethin' there, Earl!'

'What is it?'

'Can't tell yet.'

Arium scooted across the following trough. Then surged up the face of another easy passing swell. It rode the crest.

Bazza took advantage of the extra height. He rose to his feet and balanced on widespread legs. He stared ahead and to his left. Then let out a yell. 'It's a boat!'

He dropped to his knees as *Arium* swooped down the back of the swell. A few moments and they were across. Earl turned south-west. A black-hulled boat was now within easy sight. It was small as crayboats went. Bazza joined Earl at the back of the wheel-house. 'Who is it?'

'It's *Jezebel*. Karl Rick's boat.'

'The old guy who helped you when you were gettin' started?'

'That's him.'

'What's he doin' down here? Doesn't come from Cliffhead.'

'Karl gets around. Knows the water from here to Dongara, and north a good way, like the back of his hand.'

'Can't see anyone.'

Something Earl had already noticed. It was an ominous sign. 'Hope the old bugger hasn't gone overboard.'

Bazza's insides crawled. He was reminded of the decky who went down with a pot. And of his own near miss. Earl was also having bad visions.

A thought jumped into Bazza's head. 'Where's his decky?'

'Karl's got no time for deckies. Always works on his own.'

The boats closed. Water and fumes spat from *Jezebel*'s exhaust. Whatever had happened, it wasn't due to engine failure. Earl eased *Arium* alongside.

Karl was crumpled on the deck. An open plastic box lay by his hand. Flares had spilled onto the matting. Bazza gripped *Jezebel*'s gunwale and pulled the two boats together. Earl vaulted across and knelt by the old man's side. He put his fingers on the side of his throat and watched for chest movement. He glanced up at Bazza. 'He's still alive.'

'What's wrong with him?'

'Dunno.' Earl thought quickly. 'Right. Let's get him onto *Arium*.'

Bazza lightly tied the boats together and swung across to help Earl. They lifted Karl's small body and manhandled him over as gently as possible. They carried him into the wheelhouse and stretched him out on one of the two bunks up for'ard.

Earl looked at Bazza. 'Reckon you can take Karl's boat into our moorings?'

Bazza's thoughts flew apart. What? On his own? He panicked. There was reef out here. There were no street signs, or streets. Cliffhead was over there somewhere. How was he gunna find it? Then resourcefulness, acquired from his street days, took over. Even so, he felt less confident than he sounded. 'Think so. Why?'

'If we go back into our moorings, we'll still have to get Karl ashore. Then into the ute and drive up the coast. Be quicker if I head straight for Denison. We're nearly half way there as it is. I'll get Ted on the blower. He'll have the ambulance on the jetty.'

Bazza nodded. 'Makes sense. What do I do when I get in?' If I get in he thought.

'Hook onto our moorings. We'll sort it out when I get back.'

'Okay.' Bazza swung onto *Jezebel*. Slipped the ropes and pushed off. He saw Earl talking on the two-way as he put *Arium* into gear and roared off to the north.

As Bazza watched him go, icy loneliness formed inside. It was a feeling he'd known often as a child, the pain of abandonment, of not knowing to whom to turn. He was in the middle of nowhere. On a strange boat and with only a general idea of where the anchorage was. The hollow inside him expanded. He was shit scared. Then came a surge of bitterness. How could Earl drop him in it like this?

Anger gave way to reason. Constructive thoughts arose. In the months they'd been together, Earl had never been malicious. He must have a reason for doing what he had. Well, he'd handed Bazza the hot potato. It was up to him to get on with it.

Okay. What would Earl do? First things first. He pushed the gear lever into forward and slowly opened the throttle. The boat answered and shouldered through he water. He swung the wheel and headed south.

It took him a while to figure out the compass. It went the opposite way to how he reckoned it should. Until he realised he was moving the boat's bow, not the compass needle. The needle remained stationary. Not that he needed the compass. He had only to stay outside and parallel with the line of breakers on Big Horseshoe to his left.

He ploughed roughly south until he came to the end of them. Then continued a bit further to be sure he cleared anything lurking just below the surface.

The water changed colour. Browns and greens of weed covered rock or coral were no longer visible. He turned east.

The sun was now a couple of hours high. He looked under the fireball, scanned the shore and picked out the limestone hill with its cut off front facing the sea. It wasn't very big but on the featureless stretch of coast, it was a point worthy of notice. He headed straight for it. He knew there were no reefs between Big Horseshoe and those right on the shore.

Bazza opened the throttle. *Jezebel* surged ahead. The roar from the exhaust was strong, though not as powerful as *Arium*'s. The boat responded quickly to the wheel. She was a fraction more lively than Earl's. Bazza wondered how it would behave in a southerly or beasterly easterly. Probably not as well, but its owner obviously made a crust with it.

Bazza felt an affinity with the boat. A few months earlier he wouldn't in his wildest dreams have thought such a thing was possible. He, Barry McPearson, in sole command of a crayboat! At sea!

With *Jezebel* at full throttle, he realised she wasn't as fast as *Arium*. With the realisation came some understanding of Earl's decision to transfer Karl to his own boat and charge off. Time was important.

As the coast became clearer, he recognised details of the anchorage. Suddenly he knew why Earl asked him to find his own way in. If he followed *Arium*, he would be left behind in water about which he knew absolutely nothing.

The knowledge made him realise how slow he'd been at taking it all in. Earl had sized it up in seconds, decided on the best course of action. He also had confidence in his crewman. Bazza expanded. He wasn't a load of crap. He was a person. One who could think for himself. Jeez! Why had he crept around in back alleys for so long?

The anchorage was close. He reduced speed and studied the area around the shack. He was glad he'd watched Earl line up things on the shore. Street life had made him observant. You had to keep an eye on what was going on around you. Keeping tabs on where you'd been, as well as where you were going, could spell the difference between escape or getting cornered.

He spotted the two small floats marking the outside and inside ends of the way in. Crystal clear water made them redundant. He could see the reefs and the sandy channel between them. It would be a different story when the water was full of stirred up sand and weed. He cut the throttle further so he just had steerage and burbled into the anchorage.

Next, pick up the moorings. Get it right Bazz. Don't stuff it up now! He coasted alongside, slipped the gear into neutral and gaffed the rope in front of the dinghy. He swung up past the side of the wheel-house and onto the tiny foredeck, dropped the looped end of the chain over the mooring bit. He'd done it!

Pride and achievement surged through him. Six

months ago he hardly knew one end of a boat from another! He couldn't wipe the grin from his face as he swung back to the main deck and studied the controls. It didn't take long to work out how to shut off the engine. It cut into silence. Bazza stood for a moment and absorbed the peace and gentle buoyancy of the boat. Then he climbed into the dinghy and rowed ashore.

He cooked a couple of whiting and ate an early lunch. It was a long while since breakfast. Then he tried to read one of the books he and Earl bought in Geraldton. He'd progressed well with Earl's help. If he got stuck on a word, or sentence, his skipper helped him to work it out. He never belittled him for being slow. He just explained everything matter of factly, as though it was the normal thing to do. Bazza guessed it was because he'd 'been there, done that.'

He couldn't settle to it. His mind strayed. He finally gave up and walked down to the beach. On *Jezebel* he tied the dinghy so it trailed astern.

Time went unnoticed as he examined the boat from bow to stern, both above and below deck. He finally sat at the stern and just looked at it. The sun was warm, the sea calm and the boat smelled of sea, fuel and the other smells he associated with crayfishing. He linked them with other things that sat well with him. One was the sense of belonging growing with each new experience. They crystallised into the previously unknown feeling of stability.

He looked up at the sound of an approaching boat. It was *Arium*.

Earl eased through the channel and pulled alongside *Jezebel*. Bazza had rope and a tyre buffer ready to tie them together. Earl looked across at him. 'Made it all right?'

'No sweat.'

'Good on ya. Knew you could do it.'

Bazza hid his pleasure. Shifted the direction of the conversation. 'How's Karl?'

'Not good. Got an update on the blower from Ted.'

'What happened?'

'Stroke.'

'Jeez. That's bad isn't it?'

'Reckon. At the moment he's paralysed down one side.'

'Poor bugger. Will he get over it?'

Earl shrugged. 'Who knows? He's as tough as an old boot. He'll probably improve, but maybe not completely.'

'How's he gunna work his boat and catch crays?'

'Doubt he ever will. Certainly not alone.'

Bazza fell silent. He looked thoughtfully at the deck by his feet. Earl studied him. Then spoke gently. 'Too soon, Bazz.'

Bazza looked up. 'What for?'

'Read you like a book. Probably because I would've felt the same.'

Bazza felt the euphoria of the previous few hours slip down a notch. Earl tried to help. 'You gotta get your ticket first. Be another coupla years.'

'That's forever!'

'Seems like it, but it goes. Thing is, do you want it enough to do the study?'

'*Jezebel* will be gone by then.'

'Yeah. Matter of fact, someone from the factory will be down on the truck tomorrow to take it back to Denison. We'll hang it off its spare anchor in the meantime.'

'What'll happen to it after that?'

'Up to Karl. He might decide to sell it, though I doubt it. I reckon he'll at least do some line fishin'. Even if he has to crawl on board. But don't you worry, there'll be other boats. You just gotta be ready to grab the chance when it comes.'

11

Bazza tried to squash his dream. Earl was right, be patient, and ready. He pushed the disappointment deeper and looked at him. 'What about you? Still got your boat?'

Earl wiped imaginary sweat from his brow. 'Still on it, aren't I?'

'How'd you shut the bank manager up?'

'Rang him from Dongara. When I explained what happened, he agreed I'd done the right thing. Reckon his reaction would have been different if we'd gone off on a wild goose chase. Got another appointment for next week.'

'So, we live a bit longer.' Bazza was surprised at the relief he felt.

'Yep. Might even present him with an unexpected cheque into the bargain.'

'How come?'

'Landed a job while I was up there. Ted put me onto it.' Even as he said it, deep down Earl wondered why he busted a gut to get the extra job. He could have survived without it. He also wondered about a few other things he'd pushed them into.

'What sort of job?'

Earl's thoughts jerked back to the present. 'Maritime Museum want a skipper for a few days.'

'That the crowd you sometimes send critters to?'

'No. But I guess they keep in touch with one another. Might be how I got the job. Asked if I could bring my decky?' The question was obviously directed at Bazza.

Bazza's interest quickened. Why not? Might learn something. The way things were being tossed at him, it was a time for learning. He nodded.

'Good on ya, Bazz. It'll pay the bills till the crays get the moon outta their eyes.'

That nagging query again stabbed into Earl's mind. Was the real reason something else.

The next night, Earl and Bazza slept on board the *Maori*. She was a steel boat, larger than *Arium* and she was alongside the fishermen's wharf in Geraldton. They were at sea long before the sun put in an appearance.

Grove Taylor, the leader of the museum expedition had lost a day. He was frustated and edgy. Bazza got the impression the guy was up himself with his own importance. He shut his mouth and did what he was told. He wondered how Earl would handle it. Thankfully, Groves' offsider, Tony, seemed okay.

The main task was to dive on a suspected wreck at the Abrolhos Islands.

As head of the expedition Grove took the wheel himself. He was no novice with boats. He'd crewed on boats racing off the coast. Even been to the Abrolhos on previous research orientated trips, and taken the wheel.

The day's activities went well, until an evening mishap. It was sheer bad luck. Invisible in the gathering darkness, a stray pot rope wrapped itself around the propellor shaft and stalled the engine in seconds.

Not anticipating night diving, there was no under-water lighting on board. Rather than grope in the night-black water, Grove ordered the anchor dropped. The sea had been calm for days. It would only take moments to clear the shaft in the morning.

Initially, intimidated by Grove's flaunted academic achievements, Earl had shrugged, and apart from a muttered comment to Bazza about 'educated idiots,' did as he was told. A lesson learned when he worked for a sadistic skipper. His hand would be steady when he held it out for his cheque. The experience would be buried with others he'd stashed under a mental rock.

But now concern blew Earl's subservience apart. He told Grove he'd chosen a bad place to anchor for the night. Grove laid on the big boss act and overrode Earl's objections. He had investigated Earl's background. Earl hadn't even finished secondary schooling. And he couldn't be much of a fisherman if he needed work in a short lull in the cray season. He didn't even regularly fish this area, but worked somewhere down the coast!

If he hadn't been pushed for time, Grove would never have taken Earl on. Ill health had incapacitated his usual skipper. A replacement had to be engaged. The project was well planned, with much already completed. The remaining dives had to be done *now*, before the onset of winter, or postponed for months. He knew how the bean counters in the Department viewed delays. The money would be used elsewhere.

He was hesitant but the manager of the Dongara crayfish factory strongly recommended Earl. Also, for reasons Grove couldn't understand, his contemporary at the Woodman's Point Research Centre endorsed the recommendation.

The regulations were clear. There must be a qualified skipper on board. Among other things, the boat's insurance would be void if he ignored them. Well, Earl held the necessary tickets. Grove checked with the Marine and Harbours, *and* the Fisheries Department, but that still didn't mean he had to take orders from Earl.

The muted scrape of steel on rock exploded Earl into

full wakefulness. His eyes snapped open as his feet hit the deck. One leap and he was through the doorway into the wheelhouse. His eyes confirmed what he already knew. *Maori* was in deadly danger. He bellowed back down the short stairway. 'Hit the deck! Fast!'

Bazza, geared to quick reactions, was first on deck. The other two grumbled into motion. To begin with, they weren't crew. Grove in particular, strongly resented the order. Full of righteous anger, he stumbled on deck ready to rebuke Earl. Who did he think he was? The reprimand died on his tongue as a hillock of green water slid past the gunwale. The boat lifted, dropped, checked as the keel hit bottom. The crunch scattered Grove's thoughts.

Earl snapped further orders. 'Grove! Tony! Grab the spare anchor, shackle it to the heavy rope. Bazza, give me a hand with the dinghy.'

Bazza leapt to obey. Earl knew more about what to do than he did. In the same instant he wondered how the 'General' would react. He was interested to see how it came out. He put his money on Earl.

Grove pulled his thoughts together. He *was* expedition leader. He opened his mouth to register a sharp protest. Earl wasn't there. He was at the stern, unlashing the dinghy from its davits.

Tony headed into the cabin. He dug out the anchor and rope stowed up for'ard. He was used to taking orders and smart enough to realise this was no time to argue.

Grove looked around. Grey dawn wedged the darkness aside. The sea had stirred during the night. Building swells now humped onto the waiting reef. Breakers crashed a short distance to the north. Icy talons clawed at his stomach. Late yesterday, the sea was a mill pond.

Grove joined Earl at the stern. 'We will not abandon this boat!'

'Abandon nothin',' Earl growled. 'Get in.' He gestured towards the dinghy's bow.

Grove tightened his lips. Bazza could see he wanted to assert his authority but didn't really know what to do. He grudgingly climbed into the swaying dinghy. Bazza didn't need to be a mind reader to guess what he was thinking as he stared at the green waves humping and pushing towards the reef. They made Bazza's bowel quiver. They weren't breaking. Yet! But even to his inexperienced eye, their translucent quality indicated they were close.

Earl slipped the last lashing from the dinghy. He and Bazza lowered it into the water. He sprang over the stern and landed astride the central seat. His commands were sharp and clear. 'Undo that for'ard lowering rope but hold it!' He released the stern rope as Grove fumbled to untie the one at the bow. Looking down on them from the *Maori*, Bazza thought Grove looked as though he'd eaten lemons. He grinned and went for'ard to help Tony.

Earl settled by the nine horsepower motor clamped on the transom. He adjusted the controls and pulled on the starter cord. The engine burst into life and he gave it a mental pat. The last thing he needed was a cantankerous outboard motor. 'Let's go!'

Earl gunned the dinghy away from the stern. *Maori* was stronger than *Arium* but no boat likes being battered on a reef. He curved the dinghy around and came alongside. As it zoomed up and down the passing swells, he looked across onto the deck. Bazza and Tony had the anchor shackled to the rope and ready on the gunwale. Earl eased in the dinghy and directed his order at Grove. 'Hold her in!'

Grove pinched his mouth tight and struggled to hold the dinghy to the side of the pitching vessel. Earl, Bazza and Tony manhandled the anchor into the dinghy. The spare anchor was larger than *Arium*'s. If dropped, a fluke could easily hole the aluminium dinghy. The transfer was successful.

Earl gave Bazza last minute instructions. 'Make the end of the rope fast to the mooring bit. Pay it out as we go. Give us the nod when it's gone.'

Bazza nodded. Earl needed him to do it right.

Earl eased the dinghy away. Free from scrunching and thumping against the plunging hull, it pushed up the slope of a looming green hill which bore down on them like an express train. Close to the surface, the swells looked even bigger.

Grove glanced at the young man in the stern. Earl's hand was on the engine's tiller, his eyes on the sea and the trailing rope. If a rope of that size fouled the propeller it would snap the sheer pin like a carrot. Although the drag tried to slew the dinghy broadside on, Earl looked as though he knew what he was doing.

The dinghy punched over the swells until the worst of the green humps were behind them. The rope tightened. Earl looked back at the *Maori*. Straddle legged on the foredeck, Bazza waved both arms.

Earl cut power. The dinghy swung broadside on to the swells. It rocked dangerously as he and Grove bundled the anchor over the side. It clanged and thumped on the aluminium and disappeared.

Minutes later they were back on the foredeck with the others. Since that first scrape of the keel, *Maori* had moved further over the reef. Each passing trough crunched the keel more solidly on rock and coral. Grinding screeched through the steel hull. It could be felt as well as heard.

'What happened to the main anchor?' Grove asked.

'Dragged. Not enough scope. Or poor holding. Or both.'

'Same thing might happen to this one.'

'One way to find out.' Earl partly undid the end of the rope but left a couple of turns around the mooring bit. He handed the end to Grove. 'We'll pull. As we get slack, you snub it.'

Tony and Bazza grabbed the rope in front of the mooring bit and heaved.

'Wait for it. Time it with the swells.' Earl joined them and stared at the water ahead. A green mound swept towards them. The boat lifted. 'Now!'

The three of them laid into it. The swell passed beneath the boat. It peaked and nearly broke. The bow slewed. *Maori* dropped back and lay angled to the waves. Grove hauled in several metres of slack, then snubbed the rope as it grew taut. His eyes looked big. 'What happened?'

'Anchor wasn't set.'

Another swell humped through, foamed only metres behind the transom. The boat straightened. Earl gripped the rope. 'It is now! Right, on the next swell.'

Timing it carefully, they sneaked a metre of rope and snubbed it. With each succeeding wave they pulled a little more rope around the mooring bit. The bow edged seaward.

Ignoring the scrape and grind growling from the boat's bowels, the men prepared for yet another gut wrenching pull. A bigger swell loomed. Earl waited. The swell rolled through. The boat came alive, lifted its keel. 'Now!'

Two metres of rope slid around the mooring bit. The keel jarred onto the reef. Another wave lifted it. More rope slid around the bit. The next jolt was less severe. Metres of rope slid around the bit as each swell passed. *Maori* no longer hit bottom.

Eager hands pulled until she was over the original anchor. Earl secured the rope as Tony and Bazza hauled it to the surface and manhandled it over the bow. It was heavier than the spare and their backs grizzled as they carried it back to the main deck.

Bazza sucked a jammed finger as he and Tony leaned against the wheelhouse and regained their breath. The immediate danger over, the four of them reassessed the situation.

Earl and Grove remained on the foredeck. Both looked aft at the swells. White showed at the tops of some of them. They were close to breaking. The boat was barely clear of them. Grove looked at the taut rope running over the bow. 'Right. Let's pull the boat further forward.'

'Not yet.' Earl looked at the chain running from the anchor on the main deck to the foredeck and down into the chain locker.

'Why not?' Grove was suddenly aggressive. 'If we stay here, the sea has only to increase slightly and we'll have waves breaking over us.' He glared at this young man who challenged his authority.

'That's right. But if we haul in more rope, we'll lift the new anchor and be back where we started, bashin' out our behind on the reef.'

Grove bit back a retort. He was still angry, but hesitant about ignoring more of Earl's advice. He hated to admit it was sound. When he spoke, he hadn't quite stifled his real feelings. There was an edge to his voice and the words came out like extracted teeth. 'All right. What *do* we do?'

'We've got two choices, cut the rope from the

propeller shaft so we've got power, or run the main anchor further out with the dinghy and pull forward on that.'

Grove forced out the next question. 'Which do you recommend?'

'Be difficult to cut the rope off with the stern rearin' up and down like a pile driver. I think our best bet is to run the anchor further out. We can fiddle with the rope when we've got more sea room.'

Grove's nod was short and stiff. 'That main anchor is heavy. Can it be handled with the dinghy?'

'Won't be easy …' Earl called back to Tony. 'While the rest of us get the anchor organised, Tony, nick below and see if we're takin' water. Feels a bit sluggish to me.'

Tony went. Below the main deck, and at the front of the wheelhouse, up for'ard where the bunks were, a small door led back into the engine compartment.

'Okay. Let's get the anchor loaded.'

They had barely started when Tony shot from the wheelhouse. His eyes said it all. His words confirmed it.

'Bloody hell! There's water everywhere!'

12

Earl shouted orders and lunged for the doorway. 'Tony! Hand bilge pump! Bazza! Get the back hatch up and start bailin' with a bucket! Grove! Get ready to start the engine! I'll check the water level. See if it's safe to run it.'

Grove snapped back at him. 'What about the rope around the shaft?'

'We can run the engine without putting the prop in gear.' Earl disappeared.

Bazza and Tony leapt into action. Grove moved into the wheelhouse and stood in front of the control panel. He baulked at actually holding his hand poised over the starter button. His antagonism towards Earl still rumbled. It subsided when he saw another hump of green water climb in front of the bows. He could almost see through it. He lifted his hand and held it over the starter button.

A disembodied voice speared from the engine room. 'Hit it!'

Grove stabbed at the button.

Below deck Earl squatted in water already over half a metre deep. The engine rumbled into life. Water surged with each pitch of the boat. He rechecked. Nothing vital was below the surface. A sump full of water would spell disaster.

Submerged pulleys and belts sprayed water as the engine settled to a steady beat. The water was mired with spilt oil and distillate. Acrid odours bit into his nostrils. He yelled towards the small door. 'Yank on the bilge pump!'

An additional belt at the front of the engine spun into life, added more spray to the slop. Earl ignored it and moved to the rear of the engine. He groped in the water. No cold water jetted from the shaft's packing gland. Good. The propeller shaft hadn't taken a beating — yet!

Grove crawled through the doorway. His fastidious movements reminded Earl of a cat picking its way through mud. He squatted in the water just inside. 'Are we gaining?'

The clank of the hand bilge pump could be heard above the engine noise as Tony pumped up and down on the handle. At the rear, light flowed in where Bazza had lifted the small hatch. A green plastic bucket appeared and disappeared with surprising speed. Earl grinned. It brought to mind a saying among boating people that the most efficient bilge pump was a frightened man with a bucket.

Earl studied the water. It slopped and surged, coating everything, including himself, with a layer of thin black oil. 'Think we're holdin' our own.'

'What can we do?' Grove was close to hysteria. He was scared of being below deck with water pouring in somewhere. How much could the boat take before it took the big plunge?

'Find where it's comin' in.'

'Could be anywhere!'

'So? Start lookin'.' Earl moved around to the other side of the engine. 'Could be the raw water intake. Or the echo sounder's transducer. Anywhere somethin' pierces the hull. Don't think we were on the reef long enough to chew a hole in the hull, but we might have knocked somethin' off.'

Grove's eyes took on a wild look. Earl recognised the onset of panic. He snapped instructions. 'Feel in the water on your side. About level with you now. Run your hand down that thick hose. Should find a wheel valve.'

Grove put his arm into the murky water. Oily scum splashed into his face. He jerked clear. 'It's rising!'

'So what? Check that tap!' Earl's voice was harsh.

Grove's voice rose. 'The engine! If the water rises any further it'll blow up!'

'Belt up and look for the leak.' Earl groped deeper into the water on his side of the engine. He felt beneath it, as close to the keel as he could reach.

Water slapped against the red painted engine in front of his face. A few more centimetres and it *would* drown. Just as well it was a diesel. A petrol engine would already have stopped. He shut the thought from his mind and continued groping.

Grove located the tap. He was twisted sideways to try and keep his face clear of the oily water. 'Got the tap!'

'Any water coming in around it?'

Grove paused and groped. 'Can't feel anything.'

'Must be okay. then. The rate we're fillin' up, you'd feel if it was comin' in there. Hang on! I've found it!' Earl felt a stab of cold spear through the warmer bilge water. He traced it with his hand and found the cable leading from the echo sounder. The transducer had been smashed off on the reef. It had left a round hole about five centimetres in diameter. The brass fitting that normally sealed it, and carried the cable, was angled crazily in the hole. Earl wriggled it out and jammed his heel over the hole. He straightened as best he could.

'I've stopped it. For the moment.' He looked at Grove. 'Get up top. Find a round piece of wood about six centimetres in diameter. Taper it on one end.'

'Where will I find something like that?' Grove steadied himself with a hand on one of the deck beams that arched overhead. His eyes still looked big.

'How the hell should I know? Hack the end off an

oar! Tear somethin' off the boat if necessary!'

Grove headed for the small door.

'Don't forget to taper it!' Earl shouted after him. 'And tell Bazza and Tony to get the anchor into the dinghy. Main pump should handle the water now.' He then concentrated on holding his heel tight against the rush of water. The hole was in an awkward position. His muscles soon ached. He looked around. The level was hard to judge. The water never stayed still long enough.

The engine rumbled on. Its heat could already be felt. Rivers of sweat dribbled down Earl's face. He didn't think the level was rising. Could even be falling. He certainly hoped so. If it wasn't, there must be another hole somewhere.

Grove returned. He carried a piece of wood, roughly round in section. Blood oozed from a cut on his hand. He passed the wood to Earl.

Earl studied the smaller end. It was about the right size but was irregular. He dropped the wood and stripped off his shirt. He grabbed the bobbing piece of wood and covered it with a double thickness of cloth.

He hunkered down, shifted his foot and rammed the wood into the hole. It was a loose fit at first but he screwed and pushed until it was tight. He hoped the wood would swell.

He panted from exertion and heat by the time he finished. But he was satisfied. He again studied the water level. It was lower. 'Right. Let's get topside.'

He nudged Grove towards the door. They wallowed through the water like a couple of arthritic ducks. Oily smears marked the stairs as they mounted to the wheelhouse.

Earl glanced over the stern. Swells still peaked towards the reef. He joined Tony and Bazza at the side. The anchor was loaded. It had been a battle and the dinghy carried a number of shiny new dents.

Earl and Tony set the heavier anchor further out than the spare one. The dinghy shipped a lot of water but stayed right side up. Tony bailed on the way back.

On the foredeck, Bazza and Grove hauled in about half the length of the chain and put a healthier gap between the stern and the breakers. The spare anchor was lifted on board and stowed on the main deck. With luck, they wouldn't need it again.

The struggle with the anchors brought them valuable time and distance. They could now tackle the rope around the shaft. But first, Earl shot below to check the plug. The water-swelled wood was as tight as though hammered in. The water level was down and dropping. He returned to the deck.

Grove looked the question.

'It's holdin'. Don't know how it'll go while travellin'.' Earl paused in thought. Then looked up. 'I could make a patch. You could bolt it on while you're over the side.' His voice was easy, less assertive. The crisis had passed.

'How can we drill holes in the hull?' Grove asked.

'Already got a hole. All we need is one bolt and a solid patch inside and out. Two pieces of marine ply, thick rubber, whatever we can lay our hands on. We'll be mobile. Get us back to Geraldton.' He gestured over the side. 'After you've finished the job. Be pea soup shortly.'

Grove nodded. He was well aware of how quickly a swell reduced visibility. He turned to Tony. 'Get the diving gear, Tony. This is our field.'

Bazza followed Tony into the wheelhouse and they came out with two scuba tanks. Tony and Grove stripped down and helped each other into their gear.

Earl beckoned to Bazza. They returned to the wheelhouse and fossicked around.

As Grove prepared to slip over the stern, Earl offered him a hacksaw he'd found in the toolbox. It was rough with rust but tools on board a boat soon acquired such a coating. A swim in the sea wouldn't improve it but this was not the time to worry about that. 'You'll want this. That rope'll be as tight as a banker's fist. Friction melts the stuff. Goes like steel.'

Grove patted the knife strapped to his leg. 'This will fix …' He stopped. Looked at Earl. Their eyes met. Grove gave a slight nod and accepted the hacksaw. 'Thanks. You know more about ropes than I do.'

Bazza noticed the change. They'd sorted something out. He wasn't quite sure what, but he'd think about it.

Grove's voice was easier, less demanding. 'What about a patch for the hole?'

Earl offered an irregular shaped piece of marine ply. It was about a centimetre and a half thick and roughly twelve centimetres square. A one centimetre thick bolt protruded from a hole in its centre. There was a large steel washer beneath the head of the bolt. 'Bazza and I knocked it up. She's rough but honest.' He held up a similar piece of wood and the nut for the bolt. The bolt was a bit long but he had an assortment of larger nuts and washers to take up the slack on the inside. 'You wanna tackle this first? Or after you've cut off the rope?'

Tony glanced at his boss. 'Perhaps I should take care of it first, before we drop it or something?'

Grove nodded. Earl looked at Tony and continued. 'When you're in position, knock on the bottom. I'll yank out the plug. You slap that on and hold it while I put the wood on this side and tighten the nut. Okay?'

Tony nodded and both divers held onto their goggles and dropped into the water.

Fifteen minutes later they were back on board. Grove looked at Earl. 'You were right.' He lifted the hacksaw slightly. 'Without this, I'd still be down there sawing away with my knife. The rope had welded itself into a solid block.'

He became business like. 'Right, take the wheel please Earl, and take us back to where we were yesterday. Tony and I are already geared up. We'll get stuck into it before the water gets too dirty.'

Earl nodded, his manner easy and friendly. 'Sure thing. Bazza'll knock us up some breakfast.'

Bazza looked surprised, then grinned. 'You're game.'

As he headed for the small galley, he thought he had the business between Earl and Grove sorted. They recognised and accepted each other's ability. Was that called tolerance? Anyway, it was the way he described it to himself. You didn't have to be the best, just do whatever it was as well as you knew how.

Bazza felt warm confidence as he foraged among the galley's pots and pans and came up with a large frypan. He mightn't be good at anything in particular, but he was a hell of a lot more useful here than in the city.

The exploratory work was completed. Grove established that the rumours of another Batavia-like shipwreck were unfounded. At least in the reported area. He and Tony found some unusually shaped rock, covered in coral growth, but they were not a wreck. He was disappointed. Finding a new historical wreck would put his name at the top. A requisite for quick advancement in the job. However, there would be other opportunities.

Nothing untowards occurred on the trip back to Geraldton. Earl repeatedly checked the makeshift patch but it held firm. Grove was still reserved but the four parted on good terms. He assured Earl he would put in a good word for him. If another job coincided with the closed season, or a slack spell, he'd be happy to have him on board.

Earl thanked him, pocketed his cheque and made plans to head for Cliffhead. The swell would have stirred the crays. Unfortunately, there was one important call to make. Might as well get it over with. He wanted the coming days clear to work at pulling his pots. When cleaned and rebaited, the catching would be good.

Bazza was as nervous as a back alley cat as he waited for his skipper. When Earl finally stepped out of the bank the question leapt off his tongue. 'How'd it go?'

'He'll wait a bit longer.'

'Cheque help?'

'Sure did. Wasn't easy to pick, but I swear I saw his face crack.'

Bazza felt his body relax. They were still in business. He was surprised by his use of 'they'.

When they were seated in the ute, Earl stared through the windscreen. 'Sorry I dragged you into that mess, Bazz. Thought I was doing it for the best.'

Bazza's eyebrows rose. 'How do you mean?'

Earl's answer came slowly as he thought about it for long moments. 'Guess you've noticed, I've pushed you a bit ...'

Bazza looked mystified. 'That's crayfishing isn't it?'

'Yeah, but I've been bending over backwards to … teach you. Put you in different situations. More than the norm. Compact your learning.'

Bazza studied Earl for a moment. 'Wondered about that. Why?' He hastened on. 'Not that I'm knocking it! No one's ever helped me before.'

'Why! Took *me* a while to understand. My Dad's a go-getter real estate agent. Very bright. Very successful. So are my older brothers. Okay, so I was slow at school. But if someone had helped me, instead of knocking me, I'd have got it too!'

'You know a heck of a lot about boats.'

Earl nodded. 'All learnt at my own pace, and under my own steam.' He looked directly at Bazza. 'By helping you, I think I was trying to kill a few personal ghosts. But, it's more than that now.'

Bazza swallowed. Stuck out his hand. 'Ghosts are for people who've got time to think about them. I'd rather be practical, like you.'

13

The pots were a mess. Old hock bones, the odd cray shell, some half full of seaweed, but they still managed to yield three quarters of a bag of crays. The surge in the water had definitely stirred them up. It was a long day, but at the end of it, the pots were clean and the bait baskets full.

Earl was again reminded of Old Karl's advice to 'get out and keep 'em working!' The last time Earl visited him he was getting some use back in his arm and leg but was giving the physiotherapists a hard time. Old bugger would probably growl at his pall bearers for jolting his coffin. Assuming someone could ever get him into one.

The next few weeks were good. The swell petered out after a couple of days but the waning moon, and consequent darker nights, made the crays more adventurous. The catch was steady. Bigger cheques went into the bank.

Winter approached. Cold fronts became more prevalent. They brought rough weather but the stir-ups were necessary. They copped a few hidings but the increased catches made up for it.

Then the next moon ripened. Earl wasn't worried. He wanted to try a night's line fishing anyway. As Karl always said, even if things were quiet, it didn't give you a licence to sit around on your bum doing nothing. With the year's boat payment made, Earl could relax a little, but it was better to earn a bit than go to the boozer and spend a lot. A trap some fishermen fell into. Too much spare time was a pit for the unwary.

Octopus saved from the day's pull was cut into bait sized chunks. The sea was calm. After an early evening meal they headed for the eight fathom bank. Reached it as the sun's rays disappeared.

Earl let the boat drift north along the bank. The drift wasn't the same as the run of the bank so they often drifted off. On the third return to it, they hit a patch of dhufish.

They were soon muscle weary. But although their hands and shoulders hurt, and they were puffing like fat old dogs, neither of them wanted to stop. They didn't care if it kept up all night or until they dropped.

Earl was back a pace from the side of the boat. His back bent, he hauled away as fast as he could. The heavy nylon line zipped over the gunwale. Being thick, it fell tangle-free on the deck at his feet. It had already cut a small groove in the wood. Not just from this night, but from the sum of nights past.

Bazza was doing the same thing a little further along the deck. His line was as taut as wire. Reopened splits in his fingers stung from the salt. He ignored them, other than to wish his hands were as tough as Earl's.

Earl suddenly moved forward a pace. He leaned out and lifted the line clear of the gunwale. At no time did he stop lifting. A chunky dhufish slashed at the surface as it was lifted clear. He swung it inboard and dropped it on the deck. As the fish crossed the gunwale, he experienced the evergreen surge of relief and triumph that had stuck with him ever since he landed his first decent sized fish. If it did tear loose from the hook, it was too late! He had it!

He squatted, grabbed the heavy lead sinker. A practised hit on the eyelet of the large hook freed it from the fish's mouth. He readjusted the bait as he swung back to the side. The dropped rig ran. He held the line loosely to check for foul-ups.

Bazza swung his fish inboard and squatted to remove the hook. 'Blast! It's halfway down its throat!' A delay when a school of fish were biting was the last thing they wanted.

Earl let his line run unattended. It was a long way to the bottom. He grabbed the gaff and swung to help. 'Use this.'

'How?'

'Like so.' Earl grabbed Bazza's line close to the fish's gaping mouth. He thrust the round wooden handle down its copious throat. Holding the line taut along the handle, he twirled the fish around the pole. The hook came free.

'Hey! That's cunning.'

'Seconds saved could mean another fish.' Earl was already back at his own line.

Bazza's hook was bare. He quickly threaded on another piece of octopus. Pricked his finger but hardly felt it. The kilo lead sinker zinged the line towards the bottom.

Earl's line barely hit bottom before another marauding fish engulfed the chunk of bait in its cavernous mouth. He struck, then bent his back into the long fast haul. This wasn't work. It was fire in the veins. It was the high of excitement.

His fish flapped onto the deck. It was larger than the last one. He slapped the hook from his mouth. It was bare. He jammed more octopus on and dropped it over the side. He glanced at his mate as his line sang over the gunwale.

Bazza's line was taut with strain. He heaved on it but got nowhere.

'What've you got?'

Bazza unclenched his teeth. 'Snag I think.'

Earl groaned. 'Not now. Right, let it go. We'll go round and unhook it.'

Bazza released his grip. Line zapped through his

hands like a released spring. There was plenty to spare on the foam bobbin.

Earl stopped his running line and hauled it up. Night fishing was not without its hassles but the fish prowled more by night. He hoped the hold-up wouldn't lose them the school. They had not long found them and the drift was slow. There was a good chance they'd hover over the ground for a while. He could pick it up on the sounder again but there were no guarantees. The fish might not stay. So far, they'd landed nine. All good sized ones. Earl estimated they were around the seven to ten kilo mark. A few more and they'd be laughing.

Bazza picked up his line and tried to jiggle it free. He let out a yell. 'It's movin!'

'Could be the drift.'

'Like hell! Jeez! I can't hold it!'

Earl lifted his rig over the side. Dropped it on deck. Leapt to Bazza's aid. He seized the line below his mate's hands and pulled. It didn't move. But they did hold it. The line slewed towards the stern. 'You're right. That's no snag.'

'What d'you reckon?'

'Shark. Or ray. Big, whatever it is. Just our luck.'

'Why's that?'

'With whatever it is zappin' around down there, it's goodbye dhufish.'

'Might pick 'em up again.'

'Hope so. Have to get rid of this critter first.'

'Okay. What do we do?'

Earl brought the line down and took a couple of turns around a wooden cleat. 'Wear the bugger out a bit.' The line cut the water like a knife. Light from the back of the wheelhouse lit the deck but made a mirror of the water. Mysteries lay on the other side of it.

Both regained their breath, then Earl leaned over and grasped the line between the gunwale and the water. Bazza joined him. They exerted a steady pull. A metre of line came in.

They gained a bit. Lost a bit. Bazza got more splits in his fingers. He noticed Earl was using a fisted grip that took most of the strain on the tough part at the side of his palm. Bazza matched his grip. It was easier. Even so, whatever was on the end of the line definitely didn't want to come up.

When it did, Bazza's eyes nearly popped from his head. It was a large and very angry shark. The surface exploded as its snout lashed from side to side. Razor sharp teeth gleamed in the floodlight. 'Shit! What're we gunna do with that?'

Earl let out a small quantity of line. Enough to let the shark's head back into the water. He made the line fast to the cleat. 'Leave that end alone for the moment. It bites. Let's tackle the other end. Grab a pot rope.'

Bazza scooped a spare rope from the bait tray. Earl tied a lassoo in the end and handed it back to Bazza. 'Right. Where's that gaff?' He spotted it near the pile of fish and snatched it up. 'Now let's see what we can do.'

He assessed the situation. Close alongside, the water was black. He stabbed with the gaff and hooked it beneath the shark's tail. It gripped but barely penetrated the tough skin. He lifted. The tail broke the surface and lashed from side to side.

'Quick! Slip the loop over it!'

Bazza tried. The shark threshed. Water exploded into their faces. Surprised by the strength in the tail, Bazza lost his grip. It was sandpaper covered spring steel.

Earl again struck. The tail lashed clear of the water. Bazza hung by his toenails. Excitement overrode fear. He leaned further. Lunged. Got a grip. Slipped the loop part way over the tail. He pulled. The loop tightened. He hauled back. The tail jammed up to the rail. It was barely caught.

Earl dropped the gaff inboard. He seized the tail further down and heaved. It rose a half metre or so. 'Slip the rope down!'

Bazza's heart hammered. He slackened the rope and slid it below the tail fins. He again hauled back.

Earl released his grip and straightened. 'Got him!'

'Now what?' Bazza panted.

'Hang it from the rail while we get on with our fishin'.'

'What about my line?'

'I'll cut it. Put on another rig. There's no way I'm

gunna muck around with the business end of that thing for a while.'

Bazza wholeheartedly agreed. He dragged the rope to the stern and lashed the tail to the rail. The shark threshed. 'Wowee! What a monster!'

'He's that all right. Used to do a bit of scuba diving. Lost interest since I've been fishin'. Seen too many of those things. They're at home in the water. We're not.' Earl cut the line a metre from the shark's mouth. Another dhufish rig was quickly bent on. He passed it to Bazza. 'You handled that well, Bazz. Times like that there's no time to stand around gawpin'. You gotta act. I've said this before, and I'm sayin' it again, you'll do well at this game.'

Bazza could think of nothing to say. He was thankful for the shadows cast by the light as he baited the new hook. He was beginning to accept praise. Well, almost. Still got a funny feeling in his chest.

Earl picked up his own line. 'We'll drop back and see if there's anythin' left.'

Their lines ran. Minutes ticked by without bites. Bazza's heart beat returned to normal. What a buzz! The frenzy of catching dhufish. Then the wrestle with the shark. Wow! He'd dabbled in drugs with kids on the street. This was something else. He never hit up big like some kids but he doubted any of them had ever been on such a high. This was sheer unadulterated blood-pumping excitement.

Earl's voice cut into his thoughts. 'Haul up. We'll

try another drift. Probably too far from the ground.'

Earl relocated the rocky edge with the sounder. He moved updrift of it and stopped the engine. As they let their lines sing over the gunwale, the shark threshed again. It twisted its body around and they heard a crunch on the back corner of the hull.

Bazza jumped. 'Jeez! It's comin' in!'

'Probably a bit cross. Don't think I'll go for a swim right now.'

'Don't think I'll go for one, ever! Leastways not out here.'

'He'll drown. Sharks gotta keep on the move. So there's water continually passin' through their gills. We'll haul him on board when he's lost a bit of his cheek.'

Five uneventful minutes passed. Then they both hooked something and it was a race to get their lines up. Two more dhufish flapped onto the pile. Bazza let out a yell of sheer exuberance. 'Yeehaaagh! We're onto 'em again!'

Action blurred. The fish struck as fast as they could get the lines down. Eight more fish were landed. All about seven or eight kilos a piece. Then the frenzy cut out. Earl hung on for a while then hauled up his line.

'Drifted off. We'll go back and try another drift.'

Bazza nodded. He was ready for anything. He'd never felt more alive. If this was work, roll on more of the same.

On the next drift Bazza was the only one to hook a

fish. It was of moderate size. He chiaked Earl but the latter took it with easy humour. 'Long as it's on deck. Doesn't matter who put it there.'

They tried several other promising patches but drew blanks. Earl finally called it a night. It was past midnight and the fish had to be cleaned.

Leaving their lines down, but loosely tied to the rail, Earl and Bazza got stuck into it. Earl was thorough and Bazza had got the hang of it when they occasionally fished for short spells after pulling the pots.

Not long after they started gutting, Earl's line creaked and pulled free of its slip knot. He sprang to it and landed a small shark. It was a little over a metre long and as bouncy as a steel spring. Things got lively as Bazza gripped its tail and hung on. Earl missed a couple of hits then clouted it on the head with the back of the tomahawk. All accompanied by shouts and laughter as they jumped about to keep their feet clear of the snapping jaws. What the shark lacked in size it made up for with energy.

The rest of the cleaning was completed without further incident. They then turned their attention to the larger shark. As Earl predicted, it was no longer cheeky.

It was nearly three metres long and Bazza grunted with relief when it thumped on board. Both took care to stay clear of the teeth. Even though it was practically dead, it still looked menacing. Neither wanted to contribute to its last meal.

'What're we gunna do with that?' Bazza was surprised at the size of its belly. He wondered what it had last eaten. Looked as though it would need plenty to fill it.

Earl gazed at it for a moment. 'We'll gut it then leave it where it is. Tomorrow's another day. Probably cut it up for bait. Won't be worth much at the factory and it'll save us buyin' a couple of bags of fish.' He looked up. 'Right. Let's go home.'

Bazza also looked up. They'd turned around so many times during the night he had no idea where they were. 'Where the hell is Cliffhead?'

14

Earl switched off the deck light and let his night vision return. He pointed at a speck of light. 'That's the tilly lamp I put on the roof before we left. One of Karl Ricks's tricks. Without that, we'd have to stop out all night whether we liked it or not. Damn boring if the fish won't bite. Pain in the arse if the wind comes up.'

Bazza added his thanks to Karl. With the fish gone, tiredness grabbed him. 'Right now, I reckon he's more like a guardian angel than a Dutch Uncle.'

Earl laughed. 'I hope any angels I see will be better lookin' than Karl.'

Bazza half smiled to himself. His thoughts took a step forward. He had a good teacher and was learning in the big school. 'What about Big and Little Horseshoe?'

'We're well outside 'em. We'll head south until the

light bears eighty degrees, then we're in like Flynn.'

Earl was right. The trip in was uneventful. The coast eventually loomed in the moonlight. The small cliff was a homer. Bazza picked up the marker floats with a hand held spotlight.

Despite the fishing's lingering excitement, it was nice to drop the loop of chain over the mooring bit. When the engine stopped, quietness draped them like a blanket. The water was glassy and the chill in the air made them hurry to keep warm. Bazza postponed the longing for his bed. The night's work was not finished.

With the fish on the ute, Earl drove over the bumpy track to the 'main' road. The headlights cut a swathe in front as they headed for the factory in Dongara. Three quarters an hour later they pulled alongside the ramp. By then, although the sun was still a long way from putting in an appearance, it was nearly get-up time for fishermen.

The factory sat in an island of light. One sleepy worker was on duty to watch the freezers and attend to any fishermen wanting bait at the last minute. He weighed in the catch and issued a docket. Bazza yawned. *Now* they could go home. Bed, get ready!

He dozed as they began the return trip. There would be a nice bonus at the end of the week. Line fishing share-out was a third for the boat, to cover fuel etcetera, and an even split on the rest. His head drooped and he was overcome with relaxed easiness.

It was good to know you had a mate you could rely on. He slept.

The ute stopped and jerked him from a deep sleep. He lifted his head. The shack looked unreal in the headlights. He yawned and was about to shove open the door when he realised Earl hadn't moved. He looked at him.

Earl regarded him steadily for a moment. He spoke evenly. 'You did a great job tonight, Bazz. Reckon you can stretch it a bit further?'

'What've you got in mind?'

'Pullin' the pots.'

'What! Now?'

'Be at least a bag out there. It's a workable day. Gotta use every one we get.'

'Jeez!' Bazza thought about it. Working day *and* night, even if it was a one off, was something he'd never remotely considered. Reflection told him Earl was right. The season was short. There were days when you couldn't get out. Others when it wasn't worth going. He mentally asked himself how he felt. Surprisingly, he wasn't as tired as he expected. Probably still on a high, and the short sleep also must have partially rejuvenated him. 'Okay. Let's give it a go.' Did he say that?

'Good on ya, Bazz. We'll have a quick bite to eat then get stuck into it.'

'One thing. What're we gunna do with our beds? Give 'em to the Salvos?'

Earl laughed. 'You can crash as soon as we get in. We both will, and dream of our end of week cheque.'

'Just as well. A heap of money isn't much use if you never get time to spend it.'

Earl again chuckled. 'Never fear. End of the season's not far. You'll have the best part of three months to spend your money. Go on a holiday up north. Chase a few girls. Whatever takes your fancy. I'd like you back here a couple of weeks before the start of the new season so we can get the gear ready. The time in between is yours.'

Bazza sat up straight. Busy learning the job and other things, he'd never thought that far ahead. But now? Wow! He'd have the money to do those sorts of things! Just like a real person. He thumped open the door. 'Right. Let's eat, then into it.'

He enthused over what he was going to do as they ate their breakfast and Earl smiled to himself. He encouraged him but gave him some cautionary words of advice. 'Unfortunately, Bazz, money doesn't last for ever. You'll be surprised at how quickly it goes, but ...' He emphasised his next words. 'No matter what happens, if you run out of dough, or get lonely or whatever, there is always a bed and a feed here.'

Bazza looked at his skipper. The lump in his throat had nothing to do with his breakfast. 'Thanks.' He looked quickly down at his plate. His vision blurred and he missed the last chunk of bacon with his fork. Must be going soppy or something. Happened a few times lately.

Earl lightened the moment. 'That's still a coupla months away. In the meantime, let's go empty those pots before the octopussies do.'

The pattern of daily pulls returned to normal. Except when the weather had other ideas, making it even more important to get out whenever wind and sea allowed. They experienced minor blows from passing cold fronts, but the first real winter blow came with a vengeance. Gale force winds battered the coast for three days as an intense low pressure system hovered around the south-west corner. It influenced a large portion of the state and gave fishermen some sleepless nights.

In the Cliffhead area, the murky water humped into giant swells. Earl checked his moorings at the end of each summer so he knew the shackles and chains were in good condition. That still didn't stop him from jerking awake as each strong gust shook the shack. Consequently, he and Bazza were on the beach at first light each morning. Although reassured to see *Arium* still at anchor, the state of the sea made them uneasy.

Bazza was surprised at his own concern. It wasn't his boat. Be no skin off his nose if it got wrecked. He'd walk away with money in his pocket. But even as the thought came, he knew there was more to his life. In his own way, he'd become a person. To lose that would be to lose hope. The hope that had begun to stick.

The feared nightmare confronted them on the third morning. It had been a particularly bad night. Strong wind gusts were the norm. Earl went down to the beach many times. Finally drove the ute down and tried to use its headlights. The beam was swallowed by spray, rain and blackness.

Now, in daylight, anyone could see *Arium* was dangerously close to the beach. He *had* to get on board. With the prop ticking over, he could hold the boat head to sea and push away from danger. He would do that all night and all day if necessary.

During the night, the savageness of the sea made that impossible. Bazza and he couldn't launch the dinghy and plough through the waves in the dark. All he could do was worry. And listen to the radio reports. They repeated the same message. Gale force winds with no sign of them abating in the near future.

Even in daylight, Earl doubted they could get the dinghy off the beach. The water was a mess of sand and seaweed. Waves crashed on the beach with the thickness of treacle. *Arium* pitched like an exhausted pelican. The mooring chain snatched and jerked with each passing swell. She wasn't hitting bottom. Yet.

Earl and Bazza sat in the ute to escape the biting wind. Earl's stomach knotted. He had to do something. He looked at Bazza. 'What do ya reckon? Give it a go?'

Bazza shuddered. 'Looks thick enough to walk on.'

Earl grinned weakly. 'Do a JC? Unfortunately, nothin's ever that easy.'

A gust of wind rocked the ute. It decided them. They thumped up the handles and shouldered the doors open. Cold wind raked them with damp talons. The reek of torn seaweed could almost be tasted. Piles of ripped seaweed, sticks, bleached bones, smashed floats and bright pieces of shredded rope had buried the beach.

They paused with the dinghy just clear of the surging mush. Earl secured each rowlock with wire through the hole in the bottom. He normally wouldn't have bothered. The sea's wildness made him apprehensive.

They each took a deep breath and launched the dinghy. Bazza sat on the middle thwart and gripped the oars. He was as scared as hell. He'd never been this close to a storm-lashed sea before. Or sat in a dinghy, kidding himself he could take it on. It wasn't the cold that made him shiver.

Earl studied the waves, grabbed the stern and pushed the dinghy towards a sluggish weed-filled breaker. He thought of cobblers lurking in the pea soup swirling around his feet. Stung before, he didn't want to repeat those hours of agony. Especially not now.

The wave crumped in front of the dinghy, grabbing Earl's full attention. He needed a lull to enable them to get through to where the waves were humping, not breaking.

The lull came. Earl pushed. The slurry dragged at his legs and slowed him. The dinghy plumped over one wave like a sick turtle. With the soup halfway up his thighs, Earl shoved harder. He heaved himself over the transom and threw a last bit of advice at his crewman. 'If we get rolled, throw yourself to the side!'

Bazza's confidence was decimated. He hunched his back. Facing the waves, he felt extremely vulnerable. He dug in the oars. Ripped-up weed draped the oars. Weighed them down. The blades failed to clear the surface on the backward stroke. The miss-stroke left the dinghy motionless. Panic stricken, Bazza shook the blades clear. He leaned forward to get a good stroke. No foul-ups, PLEASE!

Seated in the stern, Earl saw the waves rebuild. The lull was over. He could do nothing. The first wave slopped over the bow, plastered Bazza's back with brown and green strips of weed. Ankle deep slurry sloshed in the bottom of the dinghy. Bazza dug deep, threw his weight into a desperate pull. It was like rowing in spaghetti.

The second wave thrust the bow aside. Half filled, the dinghy wallowed like a log. The third wave rolled it.

Bazza flung himself sideways. He flopped two thirds of the way clear and disappeared in the freezing goulash. His skin crawled. He shuddered, thrashed clear and found his feet. The mess was waist deep. Solid bottom reassured him. He swore at the sea. Earl surfaced. He looked as angry as Bazza felt. Oh hell! He'd blown it!

Spluttering and angry, the bedraggled fishermen waded shoreward. Bazza was relieved. Earl's curses were directed at the sea, not at him. They were shoved from behind, then slapped from the front as backwash cannoned off the piled weed.

Clear of the surging mush they turned and looked at *Arium*. It sobered them. Bazza felt particularly downcast. 'Sorry, Earl. Really stuffed that up.'

Earl looked at him in surprise. Then gently punched him on the upper arm. 'Don't knock yourself, Bazz. I knew it wasn't gunna be a piece of cake. Don't reckon I could've done any better.' He again studied his boat. Didn't like what he saw. 'But I've gotta try.'

Bazza nearly ran. But didn't. He faced the surging mush. Earl's future depended on *Arium*. In a sense, so did his. If he got a boat, he might have to handle something like this. He quelled his quivering and forced his tongue to work. 'I'm willin'.' Even as he said it, his courage almost deserted him. If Earl hadn't stepped back into the water, he would have changed his mind. He followed. Committed, he stuck to his guns.

They waded out to rescue the dinghy. It was now right side up but full of weed and water. They plucked the oars from the clinging mush and threw them onto the piled weed. The dinghy was another matter. It was heavy and impossible to drag clear.

Following Earl's example Bazza helped him rock it. Much of its load was slopped out. After each progressive lightening, they dragged it further into the shallows. They finally overturned it and carried it clear of the water. They righted it, again set up the oars and relaunched it.

Earl chose the moment. He pushed until he was waist deep in the surging goo. Then fought his way clear of the slush and slid over the stern. He threw himself onto the seat alongside Bazza and grabbed one oar. They both heaved. The shafts curved but didn't break. The blades were again mired in weed.

The dinghy survived the first few waves. Then the sea hunched a big one. It end for ended it like a fat beetle. Earl and Bazza threw themselves sideways at the last moment. Neither wanted to be trapped beneath the overturned dinghy. It would be like trying to dive and swim through stringy porridge.

Bazza panicked. There was no bottom. He kicked and threshed but made no headway. Weed dragged at him. He went down. Fought his way up but couldn't move forward. He was going down again when a wave shoved him beachward. It passed. One foot touched bottom. He lunged. The slushy beach felt like heaven when he finally reached it. Earl was a pace behind him.

Faces set, they recovered the oars and again laboriously emptied the dinghy. Earl shivered and studied the relentless waves. He lengthened his gaze. *Arium* was closer. The wave troughs deeper. She was close to hitting bottom.

The bottom was sand, but the damage would be severe. The thought of her ending up on the beach was worse. It would be impossible to move her in the storm. She'd be full of weed and sand before you could blink an eye.

They would eventually dig her out and refloat her, but by then the season would be over. Loss of earnings would be disastrous. Cost of repairs to the hull and equipment didn't bear thinking about.

Earl felt a surge of anger. To hell with the dinghy. He stripped off his sodden shirt and waded back into the mush. 'I'm goin' out!'

Bazza couldn't move. Earl looked back at him. He knew Bazza was a novice swimmer. Even if he was a good one, he'd never ask him to tackle this lot. Or anyone for that matter. Bazza slowly shook his head. 'Sorry.' He vaguely indicated the surging sea.

Earl grinned at him. 'Don't expect you to. Just hope I can. See ya!' He turned and braced himself to withstand the rush of an oncoming wave. It passed. He waded deeper. Ducked under the next one. Push from the weed filled water almost rolled him. He staggered but kept his feet. He dragged weed from his face and struck out. It was like swimming in mud.

He dived beneath the next wave. A heavy, torn up cabbage weed plant plastered his shoulder like an overgrown octopus. The water dragged on it, pulled him back. His right arm got entangled in its long fronds as he tried to push it off. He twisted and kicked.

15

He fought. Surfaced at the back of the wave. Gulped damp air. Finally dragged off the clump of seaweed. The acrid stench of the stirred up mess bit into his nostrils. It stung his eyes. The struggle drained him, sapped his determination. He caught a clear picture as *Arium*'s bow surged skyward. The taut anchor chain jerked. The bow dropped. She moved backwards.

Spurred on by the glimpse, he again struck out. The soup cloyed his skin and made it crawl. He ignored it, kicked harder with his feet. His arms dragged. Frustrated and desperate, he was forced to swim in slow motion.

Another wave reared over him. He dived and pulled into a foetal position. Almost gave in. Then he lashed out with his feet. Give in nothing! *Arium* needed him!

He surfaced at the back of the wave, paused, tried to tread the slushed water. Surge dragged him towards the beach. He again struck out. Another wave crunched down on him. There was no let up.

He dived, dredged up reserves of will power. He surfaced and again struck out. *Arium* was tantalisingly close. He ducked his head, dived through another wave. Wishful thinking? Or was the water less soupy?

He ploughed on. Yes, his arms were freer in the water. It was easier to kick. He was through the worst of it! He looked up. He had closed the gap.

He slogged alongside. The boat reared like a vicious horse. Earl trod water and judged his moment. If he missed, she'd plunge down on top of him.

He swam to mid-deck where the rearing and plunging was less marked. He waited. Grabbed. Shot a hand into a scupper. He hung on. His chest crashed against the side. He shut his mind to the pain and timed his moves. He shot his other hand up, gripped the gunwale. Another lunge and he was draped over the scarred woodwork. One more and he rolled over the side and flopped onto the deck. He lay and felt nothing.

The hard deck breathed life into him. *Arium* needed him as badly as he needed her. Energy stirred. He rolled onto all fours. Staggered to his feet. Lurched to the wheelhouse as the deck bucked. He pressed the starter button. Thankful he never left the boat without getting it ready for the next morning's start.

The engine roared into life. Vitality trembled through *Arium* and was transmitted to Earl's exhausted body. He could have kissed her. He engaged forward and eased open the throttle. The prop screwed into the water. The anchor chain sagged as the boat crept forward. Earl felt easier. There was a fraction more water beneath the keel.

His mind raced. The boat was still too close to the beach. How much longer would this weather last? How bad would it get?

He switched on the radio. The answers might lie in the next weather report. In the meantime, he'd drop the moorings and head outside. Beyond the reef was open sea. The waves would be less aggressive. With the prop ticking over he could hold position and stay head to wind and waves.

Earl gave the engine a burst. The boat surged ahead. The chain slackened. He flicked the prop out of gear and bolted up onto the foredeck. He struggled a metre of chain on board. The bow zoomed up another wave. The chain snapped rigid, tore the links from his grasp. He barely got his hands clear before it slammed on the fairlead.

Arium wrenched at the anchor. She sagged back. Earl spun around and stared over the top of the wheelhouse. The beach reached for the stern.

He swung back to the main deck and slammed the prop in gear. The boat clawed away a fraction. He adjusted the throttle to hold it there.

Situation hopeless. Without some slack, there was no way he could lift the chain off the mooring bit. He needed someone to hold the boat up.

He glanced back at the beach. Staying where he was was too restricting. It was a temporary solution at best. If the seas got bigger, *Arium* would pound herself to bits on the bottom. If only he could get Bazza on board.

He again looked at the beach. It was little more than a stone's throw away. A stone? He didn't have a stone but he did have a grapnel.

He dashed to the stern and scooped up a spare pot rope. Seconds later he was back at the wheel. He eased the bow back into the waves. A couple of seconds was all it needed. The boat payed off and headed to the side. The chain would pull her straight again but she'd be close to smashing on the bottom. See-sawing back and forth could only hasten the dragging of the anchor.

Earl tied the light grapnel rope to the end of the pot rope. He looked at Bazza and yelled above the shriek of the wind. His voice carried to the beach. 'Need you! I'll throw a line! Tie it to the dinghy! I'll pull you through!'

Bazza's shouted reply was blown away by the wind.

Earl thought a moment then again shouted. 'A thumbs up if you're willing to give it a go. It's up to you!'

Bazza shivered and hesitated. He looked at the sea. It frightened the hell out of him. He'd witnessed Earl's struggle. If he got tossed out, he'd have 'Buckley's'.

He wanted to help but was scared stiff. Thoughts chased through his mind. True, he'd experienced the greatest learning period in his life. Was this another lesson? Probably, but did he need it? He doubted it. Fat lot of good it would do him if it was his last! He started to signal, no, when a stronger thought overrode the others.

Only one person had ever told him he was useful. That he was needed. Earl! And right now, Earl needed help. Badly! He, Bazza, was the only one who could give it to him. After all the help he'd received, what sort of a bastard would he be to turn his back and walk away?

His hand rose almost of its own accord. He gave a thumbs up.

Earl tied the rope to a winch stay. He headed *Arium*'s bow into wind and waves. Then he let go of the wheel and dashed to the stern. He put every ounce of energy into the throw. The grapnel soared shoreward.

He didn't wait to see where it landed. He raced back to the wheel and spun it hard. *Arium* corrected her sideways lunge. He looked over his shoulder. Bazza was thigh deep in the water. He had the rope.

Earl nodded as Bazza struggled back through the surging mess and tied the rope to the dinghy. Good!

The youngster was all right. Earl wouldn't have blamed him if he'd chucked it. He was one gutsy kid.

Shivering and shaking, Bazza pushed the dinghy out until he was waist deep in mush.

Earl yelled. 'Jump in! Sit in the middle and hang on!'

Bazza caught the message and scrambled over the stern. He crawled to the middle thwart and sat as low as he could. His hands locked on the sides of the dinghy. He was scared, but committed. Earl knew what he was doing. He hoped. *If* he survived, he might be like that one day.

Earl slapped the rope in the winch. It tightened, lifted from the water. Strands of weed dangled from it like drenched bunting. A wave reared in front of him and Bazza locked his eyes on it. It loomed over him as though it knew he was scared. He tightened his grip and put his head down. If it was gunna wipe him out, he sure as hell didn't want it to hit him in the face.

The dinghy forged ahead. Its bow held straight. Climbed the wave. The wave broke. Water and weed crashed over Bazza. His fingers tried to dig holes in the dinghy. The boat stood straight up. The steady pull on the rope held the bow. It teetered on the point of a backward flip. Then hacked through the crest, hobby horsed and nosed down the back of the wave. Bazza exhaled and sucked in another breath. Jeez! He just might make it!

Another wave hooded like a striking cobra. More weed and water slopped over. Bazza hung on. The dinghy climbed and plunged. Nearly half full of water it wallowed through crest after crest. Earl winched. He needed three hands. He had to adjust the steering wheel and be sure the rope didn't jump from the groove in the winch head. There was no time to coil it.

The dinghy punched through another wave top. Not so steep, it peaked behind the dinghy. Bazza's fingers ached. He eased them slightly. He was through the worst of it. The dinghy closed on *Arium.*

Earl kept winching. Bazza fended off and Earl yanked the rope from the winch. Water and weed dripped on the deck as Bazza scrambled over the side. He managed a weak grin as he made the painter fast to the rail. 'Some people don't have *any* fun.' Wind on his wet skin and clothes made him feel like he'd been slapped in the freezer. At least that was how he justified his shaking. He grabbed his waterproof jacket from inside the wheelhouse. Should keep the wind off at least.

Earl grinned back at him. Both hands were back on the wheel. *Arium* took a roller on her bows, slewed sideways. He brought her back. 'Beats nine to five in the office.'

'Yeah. Central heating and cups of coffee. Who needs it?' Bazza pulled the jacket down around his hips. 'Okay. What now?'

Earl was about to answer when the radio caught

his attention. It was the latest weather report. He held up his hand. He and Bazza concentrated. Half way through, Earl took a deep breath and let it out with a whoosh. 'Bewdy!' The intense depression was moving to the south-east.

'What's that mean?'

'Means it shouldn't get any worse.'

'It's over?'

'Not yet. But it means it's about as bad as it's gunna get. It'll go on for a long while yet but it should gradually ease off.'

'So? What do we do in the meantime?'

'Drop the moorings. Couldn't manage it on my own. With you on board, I'll nudge ahead and hold it there. Give us slack on the chain. Once you've dropped it, we'll head out to sea and ride it out. Could mean maybe twenty-four hours pluggin' head to wind.'

Bazza sounded resigned. 'Another sleepless night.'

'And that ain't all. Apart from the hard rations in the survival kit, there's no food on board.'

'Gets more interesting by the minute. This anchor draggin's gettin' to be a habit.'

'Seems like it. Dunno about anyone else but it'll never happen to me again.'

'How come?'

'This is the strongest and most prolonged gale I've seen. Thought that anchor would hold in anything. Once this lot's over, I'll get another one. Same size, and join 'em with a heavy chain. Riding chain'll come off the middle. Once that's set, it'll take a tug to shift us. BUT, right now we need more water under us. Let's drop that chain and get the hell outta here.'

On the foredeck, Bazza looked towards the area of the channel. All he could see was dirty water. He called urgently to his skipper. 'Earl! Can you see the markers?'

Earl swung up onto the foredeck at the side of the wheelhouse. He manipulated the wheel with his foot. He scanned the area. Dread soured his stomach. He knew what had happened. Wild seas had chaffed the ropes. His markers were mixed up with the mashed weed on the beach.

He had a pretty good idea where the channel was but he also knew it was not very wide. A few metres either way and he would be in big trouble. Bigger than the mess he was already in.

Bazza shared his dread. The markers had been there for when the water was dirty. This storm was something else. He looked at his skipper. 'What do we do now?'

Earl glanced at the shore. The pole he had erected was flattened. He couldn't even spot the prominent bush he normally lined it up on. It had bowed in submission with the rest of the lashed scrub.

Jeez! What next?

16

Possibilities chased through Earl's mind. Drag the anchor with the boat? Naagh. Anchor was designed to hold in anything. Well, almost anything. Taken the grandaddy of blows to shift it. And anyway, it needed to be in something solid to hold against what was being hurled against them. Another problem was the lack of manoeuvring room inside the reef, and the dirty water. If they picked up and reset the anchor, as likely as not they'd drop it on flat bottom. 'There's only one alternative.'

'What's that?'

'Somewhere in that mess there's a rocky hollow. Bit shallow, but the anchor was in it. Must've broken the edge and dragged out.'

'What can we do about it?'

Earl liked the sound of that 'we'. 'Got a lung on board.'

Bazza's eyebrows lifted. So did his voice. 'Go down in that lot?'

'Won't take long. Need you at the wheel though.'

'Hell of a risk isn't it? Isn't there some other way?'

'Can't think of one. All I know is we need the anchor back in a new spot in the hollow. And more water under the keel.'

Bazza shuddered. He was glad it wasn't him. Diving in clear water was one thing. Diving in soup was another.

His decision made, Earl put Bazza on the wheel and brought out the scuba gear. He seldom used it other than to check the hull and moorings. He slipped it on and sucked at the mouthpiece. Air flowed into his mouth. Good, it was working. He let the mouthpiece hang from its hose. 'Should be enough. I'll take a snorkel with me. If the tank does conk, I can swim back on the surface.' He waddled to the side and sat on the gunwale. 'When I get down there, nudge the boat ahead. Nice and gentle, to take the weight off the chain. When it's slack, I'll hump the anchor forward.'

Bazza nodded. Although apprehensive about Earl going over the side, he was confident he could do as he was asked. The knowledge gave him a nice feeling. 'I'll try to watch your bubbles.'

Earl nodded. 'I'll let out a big blast when I'm ready to shift the anchor.' He dropped into the water and kicked his way to the riding chain. He was relieved that the water wasn't as weed filled as in the breakers. Visibility was about a metre.

Entering a world where he couldn't see prickled eerily at the back of his neck. He ignored it and hauled himself down the riding chain. It jerked and pulled as *Arium* pitched over the swells.

He followed the chain. Kept his hands on top as it lifted and flopped. Sand and weed billowed back and forth. Surge dragged at him. He persisted and pulled himself along the chain. It lifted less as he approached the anchor. He finally spotted it, pulled alongside and grasped the shank. He inhaled deeply so he could exhale a burst of bubbles. The air cut out!

Panic seized him. Then he remembered. The tank had a cut-off, a warning. He reached around and opened the reserve. He sucked. Metallic tasting air flooded into his mouth. He had ten minutes.

He concentrated on the anchor. The fluke had dragged a groove in the sandy bottom. It was his guide to the hollow somewhere in the murk ahead. He exhaled a big breath and heard the propeller increase its beat.

The surge made it difficult for Earl to keep his feet. He planted them on the bottom, grabbed the anchor and lifted. Then slow-motioned along the drag mark. The plunging ceased but the chain was heavy to drag. He leaned forward and heaved as he settled each foot. He would have been better off without flippers.

Heavier surges swirled sand and weed. The bottom disappeared. Earl pulled and hoped for improved visibility. Distance was unjudgeable. He should have counted his steps. The anchor felt heavier. Probably because his muscles were tiring. That hollow better be close!

On his next lunge, his foot fouled an unevenness in the sea floor. The flipper folded under. He lost balance and fell sideways. The anchor crashed onto his leg and pinned it to the bottom.

He cursed. Reached for it. Got his hand under the barnacled shaft and lifted. Nothing happened. He twisted. Tried both hands. It made no difference. He was stretched out like a squirming eel. He couldn't get his body over the top to obtain enough leverage.

He fought for control. Panic he didn't need. He stopped gulping at the air. Forced his breathing into a steady rhythm. It helped relax him. Okay. So he had a problem. Perhaps he could scrape a hollow and slide his leg out.

He dug at the bottom. His fingers bit through a thin covering of sand and scraped on rock. It tore his finger tips. Well, at least he'd found the hollow. Right then he wished he hadn't.

He thought again. He needed a scraper. Something to dig with. A knife, a piece of metal, anything! Fat chance. He had nothing on but his shorts.

He glared at the anchor and fought an impulse to yell. That would achieve nothing. Except relieve his feelings. And waste air.

Air! He was forcefully reminded. The tank was nearly empty. How long had he been down? At least five minutes. How much longer would it last? He glanced up. Exhaust bubbles disappeared into the soup. Movement jerked his attention to the left. A dark shape loomed in the murk.

His heart hammered. His lungs froze. He stared, tried to penetrate the swirls of suspended sand and weed. Imagination took flight. Was it the silent hunter?

Seconds crawled by. The shape moved closer. A less murky swirl fluked through. He saw the shape more clearly. It was a large storm-torn chunk of cabbage weed.

Explosive bubbles wreathed his head as he let his breath go. Then he again sucked at the mouthpiece. The air tasted like old coins. Damn this dirty water. He hated it. There could be any number of sharks out there. One would be enough. He'd get no warning.

Earl squashed the thought. Dragged his attention back to the immediate task. His air couldn't last much longer. Then what? Would Bazza notice the lack of bubbles? Would that be too late? And anyway, what could he do? Without bubbles to guide him, he'd never find him in the murk. He couldn't follow the chain. Without a lung, he would be unable to hold his breath long enough. On his second dive, he would be unable to relocate the chain.

And meanwhile …?

The tank would run out. Instead of a rush of air

when he sucked, the demand valve would open, but release nothing. His lungs would never fill. Eventually, he'd gulp. Was drowning quick? Or slow? Did you black out in a choking, gasping spasm? Or did you linger with convulsed, screaming lungs?

Earl wrenched at his trapped leg. Barnacles ripped at his flesh. He again tried to lift the anchor. It was like trying to lift a heavy barbell at arms length. And the effort ate into his air supply. He again looked up. At the top edge of his goggles, his fair hair waved like fine seaweed. Beyond, exhaust bubbles disappeared into the gloom. A thought flicked into his mind.

In a world of storm washed air, Bazza leaned out from the side of the wheelhouse. The boat was head to wind but it was difficult to keep the bubbles in sight. They were erratic and barely visible when they broke the disturbed surface. Worry nagged. Could he have misread a signal?

His concentration shifted. The bow payed off before a large swell and a stronger gust of wind. Guilt tore at him. He increased the revs and worked on the wheel.

The bow eased back. Bazza searched. Relocated the bubbles. He fastened his gaze on them. He'd promised. He was puzzled by those bubbles … He increased the revs a fraction more and *Arium* crept forward. Bazza watched until the bubbles were right alongside. Then stared at them with an intensity that shut everything else from his mind.

Suddenly he flicked the gear lever into neutral and dived over the side. He thrashed downwards. Without goggles, he could see little. Except the bubbles. Then he spotted Earl. He also made out the anchor like a dark bar across his leg.

He grabbed the shank. Pulled his feet to the bottom. Planted them and heaved upward. The anchor lifted. He staggered forward several paces then dropped it. He lunged for the surface.

Earl rolled to his feet. Checked the anchor. It was right way up and the fluke was in the hollow. He moved it to the left where the hollow was slightly deeper. Satisfied, he surfaced alongside Bazza. Their eyes met. Earl nodded towards the boat.

On board, Earl flicked the throttle back to idle. The action was almost a caress. 'You old bastard, you sure know how to make a man work at keepin' ya.' He took a slow, deep breath. The boat was beyond the breakers. He looked at his mate. 'Thanks, Bazz. Thought Old Davey had me.'

Embarrassed, Bazza brushed the thanks aside. 'Fast thinkin' on your part.'

'Fast action on yours. Was hopin' like hell you'd know about it.'

'Read about it in one of your books. Morse code. Three short, three long, three short. SOS. Meant you were in big trouble.'

Earl held out his hand. Bazza's hand was engulfed in a strong firm grip. It lasted long moments. There was a wry grin on Earl's face. 'I reckoned we had the makin's of a good team. Man, we *are* a team. And a bloody good one at that.'

Bazza looked straight at him. He'd come a long way. He was no longer worthless. He could look anyone in the eye. He wasn't better than anyone else but he wasn't below 'em either. He couldn't quite explain the feeling, even to himself, but his mind continued to chew at it.

Thoughts solidified. The past six months had reshaped him. He'd learnt about himself. If he hadn't overcome his fear? Hadn't come out in the dinghy? If he hadn't recognised Earl's signal? If he hadn't dived down?

But he had! He was capable. He was out of the gutter. He was a person of value. He was an individual. Yet part of a team. He soaked up the feeling. Liked it.

Earl looked shoreward. The breakers still crashed onto the beach but were now at a safe distance. They didn't look as ferocious when seen from the back. Both knew what it was like to face them.

'Don't fancy tacklin' that again just yet. And anyway, be as well to sit tight for a while. See if the old girl's well and truly anchored.' He shivered and looked back at Bazza. They dripped water, and even though the wheelhouse kept most of the wind off them, enough whipped around the edges to increase the chill factor. 'Cold?'

'As a copper's welcome.'

Earl shot into the small cabin and emerged with two grey blankets. They were damp from the moisture laden sea air, but what the hell? They wrapped them around themselves and Bazza settled at the back of the wheelhouse. It was warmer in the cabin but Earl wanted to be where he could see what was going on. He took bearings on a couple of landmarks to check for drag.

They sat for a while, and gazed at the shack visible over the low sandhill. Earl voiced the thought occupying them both. 'Breakfast's a long way away. Feed of bacon, eggs and tomato would go down well.'

Bazza groaned. 'Yeah. Don't fancy one of those hocks in the bait tray.'

Earl grinned. 'You and me both.'

Silence returned. Then Earl came up with a suggestion. 'Could try those survival biscuits in the emergency kit. Reckon this is an emergency. Don't you?'

'What're they like?'

'Dunno. Never tried 'em. Look like particle board but they're supposed to be nourishing.'

Bazza looked interested. 'Guess they should be tested occasionally?'

Earl nodded and rolled to his feet. He disappeared into the wheelhouse and emerged with the kit.

They got down to some serious testing. Earl offered his opinion. 'If you crack off a piece, then suck it for a while, doesn't seem too bad.'

Bazza nodded. 'Doesn't look like it, but it does taste better than the corner of a carboard box.'

Silence again as they worked on the biscuits. They went back for seconds.

Earl spoke around the chunk in his mouth. The conversation was slow paced. Their emotions needed to slow down, and besides, they weren't going anywhere. For the present, they were content to be. 'Well, Bazz, you've had one hell of an initiation over the last six months. Wouldn't blame you if you put on your runnin' shoes, but I assure you, it's not like this all the time. Sometimes a whole season can be borin' as hell. But what d'you reckon? Gunna stick with it?'

Bazza thought about his answer. Run? Where to? Back to the city? No way! He nodded. 'First time I've felt there was any reason to life.'

Earl nodded. 'Good. Happy to continue as a decky?'

Bazza again hesitated. When he'd been at the wheel of a boat, on *Arium* or *Jezebel*, he'd experienced … he had trouble naming it. Thoughts progressed. His potential maybe? His capability? To hell with names! He bloodywell liked it!

He didn't want Earl to think he was disloyal. At the same time he felt he should be honest. It was fences down time. Nothing to hide. No cover ups. 'Right now, yes. But not forever. Kinda like to think I could … you know …'

'Way I figured it. If you've got any get-up-and-go, you try to improve.'

Silence. Earl was again the one to break it. 'Be another coupla seasons. Before you have your seatime. If we get our heads together, you could have your own boat after that. Well, the first bit of it anyway.'

Bazza wanted that, but past experience prompted caution. Better to expect nothing. When you thought you were safe, something kicked you in the guts. Lately, he had felt as safe and confident as he had ever been. To hope was to tempt fate. But to totally squash it was becoming more and more difficult. 'You reckon?'

'Yeah. You've got the intelligence. We've just gotta steer you in the right direction. Right as far as the system goes.'

'What's that mean?'

'Means conform enough to get the bit of paper saying you can operate a boat.'

'Like the sound of that. Where do I start?'

'You've already started. Learnin' to read and write.'

'How long do you reckon it'll take?'

Earl thought a moment. 'Maybe this closed season you could put in more time with your literacy teacher. The following closed season, enrol at Tafe. Get your coxswain's ticket. In between times, I'll help all I can.'

'What do you get out of it? You'll lose your decky.'

Earl was silent for a long moment. Then he spoke evenly. 'Might gain a friend?'

Bazza swallowed before he answered. It wasn't biscuit stuck in his throat. 'Reckon you've got that already.'

An embarrassed silence lingered as they both wrestled with unaccustomed feelings. Guys weren't supposed to talk like this were they? They stared at the shore. *Arium* had not drifted. If anything, the wind had shifted slightly south of west. The first real indication that the blow was past its peak.

Earl changed the subject. 'I reckon if we reversed the process of gettin' you out here, we could get back to shore.'

'In the dinghy???'

'Back it in, and use the rope to keep her bow straight on to the waves.'

'Let the rope out as we go?'

'Yeah, and hold on when a wave comes. That way we won't tip over backwards. Or slew sideways and roll. With lifejackets on, even if we do get dumped, we'll end up on the beach. Probably get wet but what the hell, you can't get wetter than wet.'

Bazza thought a moment. The trip out had terrified him but the successful outcome gave him new strength. And Earl did know what he was about. There were lifejackets on board. Even in that soup they'd float. 'Sounds interesting. Besides, I don't fancy a steady diet of these cardboard blocks.'

Earl grinned. 'Right! Let's do it!'

Eye of the Eagle

RON BUNNEY

After they witness the cold-blooded massacre of their family at the hands of white settlers, two Aboriginal children flee terrified into the bushland. They escape with their lives, but it seems nowhere is safe, and life will never be the same again

Notable Australian Childen's Book
Children's Book Council of Australia

ISBN 1 86368 126 4   RRP $9.95

Killer Boots
The Big Game

WENDY JENKINS

Two sensational footy books, charting the progress of
Greg and his favourite team, The Dockers. In these
action packed stories, footy is more than just a game,
and the stakes are as high as they get.

Killer Boots   ISBN 1 86368 138 8   RRP $10.95
The Big Game   ISBN 1 86368 183 3   RRP $12.95

Gaz

Different
Voices

Gaz Takes Off

WARREN FLYNN

Gaz wants excitement, and boy does he get it! A bike
prang, a drug bust, a big fight, and Kim — all in the first
book. The pace hots up with Kim in *Different Voices* as
she deals with her traumatic past in Vietnam. Then Gaz
takes off, and there's no holding him back. His first time
skiing and he goes ballistic! He meets two of the
spunkiest French chicks imaginable. Gets mugged in the
Toronto subway. Falls in love (again!). Could all this be
true?!

Gaz   ISBN 1 86368 084 5   RRP $9.95
Different Voices   ISBN 1 86368 135 3   RRP $10.95
Gaz Takes Off   ISBN 1 86368 180 9   RRP $12.95